International Praise for *City of Ash and Red*

"*City of Ash and Red* is a tale of survival and ruin that leaves no room for even a single drop of comfort to seep in. Pyun builds an airtight masterpiece of agony and mystery with her masterfully crafted sentences, and she colors it with the ash-gray of ruin and the fiery red of life."

—*Korea Economic Daily*

"A story of modern humanity's survival and downfall as told through the tale of a man who finds his life ruined for reasons he doesn't understand, in a city rife with disease, soiled by trash, and teeming with rats . . . [with narrative] tension like a discordant note that jangles the nerves to keep the reader hooked all the way to the last page."

—*Munhwa Ilbo* (Korea)

"Hye-young Pyun has made a name for herself in literature with her exquisite depictions of a world of strange and grotesque imagination. . . . Though the world she describes is a fictional one, the story of the extinction and denial of a weak man who must persevere within that world feels all too real."

—*Kukmin Ilbo*

"Completely astonishing."   —*Le Vent Sombre* (France)

"A dark and utterly unclassifiable novel."

—*La Bibliothèque de Glow*

"A keen (and rather frightening) meditation on identity, the vacuousness of human relationships, the absurdity of existence . . . and the instinct to survive!"   —*Zibeline*

"A dark, sometimes absurd, often Kafkaesque, fierce, and always harrowing portrait of solitude by force of circumstance and a life in freefall."   —*Le Choix des Libraires*

Praise for *The Hole*,
Winner of the 2017 Shirley Jackson Award

"A Korean take on *Misery*."
—*Time* magazine, "Top 10 Thrillers
to Read This Summer"

"An absorbing look at the struggle to find meaning in life's little passages, arguments, and disagreements."
—*San Francisco Book Review*

"By the time Hye-young Pyun's taut psychological thriller *The Hole* has tightened its grip on the unsuspecting mind, it's too late to escape. The shadows lurking in the novel become manifest, and dark poetic justice reigns. . . . *The Hole* is an unshakable novel about the unfathomable depths of human need."   —*Shelf Awareness*

"Winner of many of Korea's top literary prizes and accolades, Pyun proves to be an effectively chilling storyteller whose expert narrative manipulations should earn new followers."
—*Booklist*

"[Be] wary; you'll be thinking and dreaming this novel long after you've put it down."
—*Words Without Borders*, "July 2017 Watchlist"

"A claustrophobic, riveting story calculated to get under your skin."
—*Korean Literature Now*

"*The Hole* is rooted in character but has the suspense of a thriller. . . For readers who are unafraid of knowing that our life and our loved ones are strangers to us.
—Krys Lee, *World Literature Today*

"*The Hole* is a masterwork of suspense, and a profound meditation on grief, solitude, and secrecy. At once unsettling and richly moving, *The Hole* is a vital novel, a gift from a wildly inventive writer."
—Laura van den Berg, author of *Find Me*

"Like Hitchcock or Abe, Pyun peers head on into the unnerving depths of human grief with the most methodical of eye, logically narrating our descent into such a clear, uncanny terror we hope to remind ourselves its only just a book, one wound from end to end with an exquisite magic that refuses to let go."

—Blake Butler, author of *300,000,000*

"While reading *The Hole*, you'll find yourself suddenly doubting everything. Pyun is asking us a tough and terrifying question that none can dodge: *Is your life safe?*"

—Kyung-sook Shin, *New York Times*–bestselling author of *Please Look After Mom*

"Fissures in life offer a glimpse of the truth that starts not from others but from us and that we are all oblivious to."

—*Maeil Business Newspaper* (Korea)

"Reminiscent of Stephen King's *Misery*, Hye-young Pyun's *The Hole* shows off her unique style of steadily rising terror with this dark tale of a man utterly cut off from his life."

—*Munhwa Ilbo*

"[A] disconcerting and often sinister story."

—*Korea Herald*

편혜영

재와 빨강
270

CITY OF ASH AND RED

A NOVEL

HYE-YOUNG PYUN

Translated from the Korean by
SORA KIM-RUSSELL

ARCADE PUBLISHING • NEW YORK

FICTION
Pyun, H.

First English-Language Edition

This is a work of fiction. Names, places, characters, and incidents are either the products of the author's imagination or are used fictitiously.

Originally published in Korea as 재와 빨강 (*Jaewa Ppalgang*) in 2010 by Changbi Publishers

This book is published with the support of the Literature Translation Institute of Korean (LTI Korea).

Visit our website at www.arcadepub.com.

10 9 8 7 6 5 4 3 2 1

Library of Congress Cataloging-in-Publication Data is available on file.
Library of Congress Catalog Number: 2018025792

Cover design by Erin-Seaward-Hiatt
Cover illustration: iStockphoto

ISBN: 978-1-62872-781-4
Ebook ISBN: 978-1-62872-783-8

Printed in the United States of America

PART ONE

ONE

Danger warnings are more common than actual danger. And yet when danger does finally strike, it does so without warning. That was why the man thought nothing of the quarantine notices and infectious disease prevention regulations posted all around the airport. He knew that the more caution signs there were, the less danger he was in. As if overhearing the man's thoughts, a health inspector in a hazmat suit who was scanning the temperatures of disembarking passengers looked hard at the thermometer and gave him a warning frown. Was it the man's slight fever? The stink of alcohol wafting off of him? He clamped his mouth shut and slipped a hand up to his forehead. It felt like the lid of a rice cooker set to warm.

The flight had been short but exhausting. Not only had he been working overtime every night to prepare for this trip, he was still hungover from the night before. His hand felt even warmer than his forehead. His wrist ached and his palm throbbed as if he had been squeezing something hard. He took a closer look and saw that his palm was bruised. Even the slightest clenching of his fist brought on a tingling pain.

This time, the health inspector placed the thermometer directly against the man's right ear. An electric hum buzzed in his ear like an alarm. He barked out a loud cough as if in response to the sound, and the health inspector jumped back.

The inspections were due to the recent outbreak. An illness had been spreading fast, from country zero to most of the rest of the world, like fire jumping from roof to roof. No one knew exactly how it was spreading, treatment was still in the developmental stages, infection rates were high, and there was talk of a growing feud among countries to secure the limited supply of vaccines. And yet, luckily, there'd been few fatalities so far. The man figured the news back home was right: no matter how strong the virus was, he had nothing to worry about as long as he kept his hands clean.

On the way there, the man had been seated next to another passenger who had coughed nonstop, right up until they were lined up in the aisle to exit. The coughing man had shivered uncontrollably, despite the unseasonably heavy, old-fashioned tweed coat he'd kept on, and complained of a severe headache, swallowing three or more aspirin during the five-hour flight to Country C. The flight attendant had brought two extra blankets and covered the sick passenger up herself, and blamed it on the air-conditioning. But the aspirin seemed to have no effect on the fever, as the coughing passenger's face stayed the same deep shade of red. If the man had known how strict the airport's health inspection would be, he would have taken some aspirin himself before getting off the flight, and if he'd known how high the infection rate was, he certainly would have asked to change seats.

The health inspector gave the man a look and said something into his walkie-talkie. A reply came back, mixed with static, and abruptly cut off. Instantly, two men came walking towards the checkpoint. With their puffy suits and face masks, they looked like rubber lifeboats bobbing towards him. Their suits were clearly stamped with the words DISEASE CONTROL CENTER. He assumed they were public hygiene medical examiners attached to the airport. Their suits were identical, and they were even similar in height, which made it difficult to tell them apart. The masks covered their eyes, but the man knew they were watching him closely. His heart began to race. He did not know why but he felt he should not let them take him away. He quickly scanned his surroundings, but before he could make a move, the inspector who had checked his temperature grabbed his arm. He stood there powerless, trapped in the other man's suspiciously strong grip.

The inspector held onto his arm until the two men were on either side of him. They did not touch him, but standing there between the two large men and sweating profusely, he felt hog-tied. The other people waiting to go through health inspection and passport control stared at him. Maybe it was all those eyes on him, but his sweat turned cold and he grew so flustered that he swallowed wrong and started coughing uncontrollably until the blood rushed to his face and his cheeks burned.

The two medical examiners took him down a long, featureless corridor and into a room that looked as if it had just been dipped whole into a bucket of white paint. The floor was tiled in white, and the walls and ceiling were painted white. There was a small cot covered in white sheets, and a table and chairs that were also white. Everything gleamed like a freshly bleached and disinfected sink. All that white made the room look frigid, and indeed the air conditioner was set so low that he caught a chill and coughed several times while rubbing the goose bumps that broke out on his arms.

One of the medical examiners directed him to sit and slowly sat down across from him. The examiner's friendly, polite tone put the man at ease. He had pictured himself being thrown to the floor the moment he stepped into the room. The examiner apologetically explained that the man had an unusually high temperature and was being detained so he could receive a complete checkup. The man barely understood a word of it. Not that the examiner's choice of words was particularly difficult, but the man was not very good at the language of Country C to begin with, and he was too flustered to catch the words he did know. He stared blankly, feeling like a fish in a tank, as the examiner repeated the same words over and over, until the other examiner, who'd been standing by, lost his patience and went to fetch an electronic dictionary. Between the dictionary and a mix of speaking and writing, the man finally understood that he was being detained for quarantine. He felt a deep sense of relief that had nothing to do with whether or not he was infected.

The first examiner had him change into a hospital gown and lie on the cot, and then inspected him from head to toe, searching for symptoms of the illness. The man kept raising his head from his prone position and straining to keep track of the two examiners.

"There's nothing to worry about," the examiner said gently. "This is just a preventative measure." He seemed to sympathize with the man's anxiety.

"Preventative?"

"Yes, just think of it as a regular physical. Most of the time it's nothing, and you can laugh about it later."

"I've felt a cold coming on for some time."

"Oh, then you're definitely infected."

The man sat bolt upright in shock, but the examiner laughed and gently pressed him back down by one shoulder.

"Calm down, I'm only joking. As a matter of fact, the illness that's been going around is no different from the common cold in that they're both caused by unknown viruses. The only difference is that a cold responds to aspirin, while the new virus does not. Don't worry. Most of the people who come in here with fevers turn out to only need some aspirin."

Though he struggled to understand the words the examiner kept repeating, the man was relieved to recognize "nothing" and "aspirin." This incident would soon be just an amusing anecdote from his time spent working in Country C. He found himself suddenly craving an aspirin as if it were some delicious food. Just one aspirin, small and round as a button, he thought, would not only take away his faint headache and his cough but also cure his hangover and his anxiety.

Instead of an aspirin, the examiner held out a cotton ball soaked in alcohol. He rolled up his sleeve to make it easier to draw blood. His forearm was black and blue.

"That's an unusual color," the examiner said as he searched for a vein.

The bruises on the man's arm seemed to turn a darker blue by the minute, like a shy little girl whose cheeks turn redder the harder she tries not to blush, he thought. After several failed attempts to find a vein, the examiner finally managed to slide in the needle. Meanwhile, the man struggled to remember what had happened the night before. Had he gotten in a fight? Judging from the bruises, it was obvious someone had hit him. He'd never won a fistfight before in his life. Pure, red blood filled the syringe. He wasn't sure if it was the color of his blood or the fact that he could not remember a single thing from the night before, but something made him frown.

The results weren't ready until the next day. During his overnight detention, the man had examined the mysterious marks on his arms one by one. The stark white of the room made the blue of his bruises even more conspicuous. But no matter how he stared at them, he could not remember how he'd gotten them. It wasn't the first time he'd blacked out while drinking, but he had never woken to find himself injured. His lost memories of the night before had vaporized without a trace into his bruises, into the ache deep inside his bones, in the unexplained fear and unpleasantness he felt every time he tried to search his memory. He grimaced as he fingered the large, distinct marks and then gave up on trying to recover his memories.

It was evening by the time one of the medical examiners returned, carrying a large envelope. Excited, he nearly ran to embrace him. But he worried it might be a bad sign that the results had taken so long, so instead he greeted him in the small voice of a student who knows he is about to be scolded by his teacher.

The medical examiner handed him his clothes with a friendly, reassuring smile. He got dressed and looked over the documents in the envelope. One was a detainment consent form. It seemed unreasonable to have him sign it after the fact, but he was just happy to get out of there and hurriedly signed the paper. For the physical examination certificate, he listened to a brief explanation and signed that as well. The gist of it seemed to be that he would need a follow-up exam since it was too early to make a definite diagnosis, but for now he was released from detention and allowed to enter the country. He knew he could have taken this time going over the documents and asking questions, to understand in detail what it all meant, but the thought that he was free to leave made him suddenly anxious. The examiner put the signed documents away and asked where the man was staying. He showed him the rental contract that Mol, his contact at the main office, had sent him. Mol had included the keycard to his new apartment and a map drawn in such detail that anyone could find it easily on their first try. It showed how adept Mol was at his job, and this made the man, who was not quite so meticulous, all the more nervous.

The medical examiner dialed a phone number on the contract—to confirm that it was valid, the man assumed. He didn't know who the examiner was calling until he heard him read off the name of the branch manager back home, who was listed at the bottom of the contract as a personal reference, and ask to be put through. The man slowly folded his hospital gown as he listened in on the conversation. The name of the city and the area where his new apartment was located were mentioned, and he thought he heard something about his high temperature and about being detained, but the words he did not know outnumbered the words he did know.

He was grateful for the phone call. He'd been unable to notify the branch manager about his detainment. There had been no way to contact anyone on the outside, and anyway he was too flustered at the time to even think about the company. If not for that call, he would have been seen as a deadbeat, an untrustworthy and unreliable employee who skips out on the very first day of work. He was supposed to start that day. But right up until his arrival at the airport, the idea that something might prevent him from showing up for work never once occurred to him.

The medical examiner hung up and handed him his passport, then repeatedly told him not to change addresses or leave his place of sojourn, as he would be visited for a follow-up diagnosis. Excited to be released from detention, he forgot to ask if they knew when the follow-up would happen. He did not discover until later, after arriving at his new apartment, that next to the entry stamp in his passport was a mysterious red stamp.

The examiner also presented his black suitcase with the baggage label still attached, and said something that the man interpreted as "thank you for your cooperation" and either "take care" or "work hard." He took the suitcase with a smile. Cooperate and work hard. That was exactly what he wanted to do.

At last, he entered Country C.

TWO

The smell. It was so foul that it forced itself all the way to the bottom of his lungs and rattled his intestines. He gagged before he could get the taxi door open. The driver pulled to a hasty stop in front of the bridge. The man leaped out of the cab and vomited on the curb, long strands of sticky saliva dangling from his mouth, while the cab driver, who still needed to be paid, stood off to one side and covered his masked mouth with a gloved hand to keep from breathing in the stench. As soon as the man was able to staunch his nausea and pay him, the driver sped away, as if he dared not stay a moment longer.

The man had a difficult time catching a cab at the airport. That is, he had gotten one right away at the taxi stand. But the driver took one look at the address on the slip of paper the man showed him and sternly shook his head. Several times, the man got into a cab only to have to get right back out again, and was even refused a ride before he'd gotten the door open. It did not take long for him to realize that all of the drivers were trying to avoid District 4, where both his company and his apartment were located. Every city had its places where the roads were very narrow, or the road signs were bad, or the road conditions themselves were terrible, or there were few people around, making it unlikely for a taxi driver to get a return fare. The man thought District 4 might be one of those places.

Instead, District 4 turned out to be a lone island created from reclaimed land during the building of a river levee on the outskirts of City Y, the capital of Country C. It was connected to the mainland by several long bridges that spanned the river. But during construction, it was discovered that the island had been built on top of buried industrial waste and household garbage, and the politician who had backed the project was kicked out of office and his political career ended. As rumors spread that the island, first intended as a posh commuter suburb for the capital, was in fact a landfill, the land price plummeted, the market value crashed, and most of the residents fled. In the aftermath, it was converted into a business park with relatively affordable rents, and for that same reason, residents had slowly begun to return.

At the airport, the man had been starting to wonder if he would have to stay in a hotel instead, and he told himself he would try just one more taxi. This time, the driver took the slip of paper with the address on it and gave the man a long-winded explanation that he could not follow. The driver spoke slowly and had to repeat himself several times, but the man finally understood that the driver was telling him he could not go all the way to the address but could drop him off somewhere close. He had no idea how close was close, but he figured, once there, he could catch another taxi the rest of the way. He nodded in consent.

During the ride, the driver listened grimly to the news on the radio and did not say a single word to him. The news alternated between the urgent voices of an announcer and a reporter on scene who sounded like they were reporting the same story over and over. They talked so fast that it was safe to say the man understood exactly none of it. But that meant he could sit back and listen indifferently to the unfamiliar language as if it were only so much music and gaze out at Country C submerged in darkness. His face floated like a ghost against the lights of the city speeding past outside the window. A ghost—a disembodied being that hides its true existence. That seemed like just the right word to describe his presence in that city.

He had left his coworkers, with whom he had had a fall-ing out because they thought he had been granted special favors, and he had left his ex-wife, who had practically become a stranger to him despite having once been his clos-est friend, to come to this place, in the mood for a fresh start, confident everything would go his way, as one receiving the gift of a new life. But each time he thought about his home country, the premonition that he would never again set foot on native soil rushed over him, and he felt that he had been banished rather than having left of his own free will. His heart pounded from the muddled sensation of being an outcast and the pride of starting a new life. As the taxi passed through the dark center of the city, he raised his hand and pressed it against his strangely racing heart.

The bridge was so long that he couldn't see where it ended. The other side lay buried in shadow, as if it had been lopped in half, making it look dangerous to cross. He stared for a moment at the silent bridge, deserted of cars and pedestrians. Somewhere in the dark at the other end lay the apartment where he would live and the head office where he would work. There, too, was the him that had bidden farewell to his old exhausting life, and the him that would enjoy a vibrant solitary life with new foreign coworkers. His only regret was that all of it lay on the other side of a darkness that was as black as pitch.

He waited, but when it became clear that no other taxis were coming, he picked up his bag with one hand and wheeled his suitcase behind him. He had not packed much, but his suitcase felt heavy, as if it contained the whole world. He began crossing the bridge over the tarry water. If it weren't for the trash drifting downstream—the surface of the water was littered with garbage, as though a flood had torn through recently—he might have mistaken the river for a stagnant, festering swamp. The cab driver had dropped him off nearby as promised; according to the map Mol had sent, the bridge was an access road into District 4.

13

He had barely managed to stop his insides from churning and was almost across the bridge when he discovered the source of the smell. Piles of garbage were stacked at the end of the bridge, built up in layers like the floors of a building. What he thought in the dark was a signboard standing in front of a shop turned out to be trash, and the long building that looked like a squat military barrack in the distance turned out to be a line of dozens upon dozens of garbage bags. He didn't have to wonder long about what was scattered all over the streets, as that too was trash. There was trash everywhere—in the places he could see, of course, but also in the places he couldn't readily see. The foul odor was coming from all of that neglected trash, and the same black soup that trickled out of the garbage also oozed out of the pavement and leaked up from deep inside the earth, where the old trash lay buried.

He had heard once about a city that had problems with trash. Not here, but in some other country, a city famous for its beautiful harbor. The landfills had become saturated and sanitation workers went on strike over political issues. The uncollected garbage was left to rot in the middle of a historic city. Decomposing trash stank up the streets and spewed toxic gas, making residents ill and corroding the city's ancient ruins. A protest rally was held, and the government responded with brute force, turning the peaceful demonstration into a bloody melee. Riot police with metal batons and citizens wielding picket signs clashed among the teetering piles of garbage. Not far from the streets where the demonstrators were spilling their blood was the harbor. Seen from afar, the harbor was as pretty as a postcard. White sails bobbed gently in the breeze. But up close, the water's surface was covered with trash. Litter surrounded the sailboats and spread wide like long shadows. Maybe, the man thought, District 4 was going through the same situation.

Just as he was passing the seemingly endless row of garbage, one of the wheels on his suitcase, which had been wobbling and shaking the whole time, finally broke off. The tiny wheel rolled smoothly away and disappeared into the mountain of garbage. He decided to drag the suitcase rather than look for the wheel. The trash bags seemed to be moving and he could hear something that sounded like panting. There were probably cats and dogs and countless packs of rats digging through the garbage. They would not go hungry in this city.

Between his broken suitcase and his bag, he had no free hand to plug his nose with and had to keep breathing in the stench. But it helped him get used to the terrible smell that had tied his intestines into knots. He even stopped to look over a display of fake food in the window of a closed restaurant. Despite the trash littering the streets and the evil stench coming from it, the sight of that fake food made him ache with hunger.

All of the shops were closed. The man had read somewhere that the city council had passed a law preventing businesses in City Y from staying open past eight at night. Quality of life outweighed shopkeepers' right to survive. In fact, everyone who lived there was obligated to do more than just maintain a livelihood but to work to improve the quality of their individual lives. City Y demanded a certain level of refinement from its citizens, and for that to happen, everyone had to be guaranteed a certain amount of leisure time, regardless of the inconvenience or financial losses incurred. Though, of course, some businesses found ways to skirt the law.

The man wondered how anyone could enjoy a quality life amid this foul stench, and he questioned whether giving people leisure time automatically made them culturally refined, but ever since getting out of the cab and walking, he had realized that once you were inside the smell you stopped noticing it. Leaving the trash to sit uncollected for so long was a bold statement of the sanitation workers' rights to a quality life. Even in a city festering with garbage, a city that reeked, it was only right that everyone should enjoy a little human dignity. Walking on top of the garbage strewn across the sidewalk on the way to his new apartment, the man thought, as long as he was in Country C, he too would soon enjoy compulsory leisure, cultural refinement, and a dignified life, and he began to cheer up.

The apartment building crouched in the dark like a big, gentle dog. Relieved to have finally arrived, he set his bags down for a moment and looked up. The night sky was narrow and dark, making the roof of the twenty-five-story building look like it was being sucked into the mouth of a deep, black well. As he stood there, head tilted back, the darkness swallowed the building inch by inch.

He got off the elevator at the fourth floor and slid the keycard into the lock for apartment number six. The lock clicked open. He wanted so badly to lie down that his legs shook. His arm, which ached from dragging the broken suitcase, had turned stiff and numb. He left the suitcase in the hallway, stepped inside, and inserted the keycard into the wall slot to turn on the electricity. After a brief pause, the lights flickered on to reveal a single room, kitchenette, and bathroom—a typical bachelor apartment.

He was about to remove his shoes when a telephone rang. The sound of it gave him a start. He hadn't known the apartment even came with a telephone and of course wasn't expecting any calls. But he figured it must be the building superintendent checking to see that he had moved in, or else it was Mol, calling to find out whether he had arrived yet, so he hurriedly kicked his shoes off and thumped across the floor to grab the phone.

Just as he had thought, it was Mol. Mol spoke slowly, using short sentences and relatively simple words, to allow for the man's tentative grasp of the language, and purely for that reason, the man was able to catch most of what was said. Mol briefly consoled him on the fatigue of travel and the trouble he had gone through, what with being detained and all, and then hesitated, as if gearing up to ask the man a difficult favor, and finally said it would be good if he did not come into work for the time being. The man took this to mean that Mol wanted him to rest for a few days, as there would no doubt be a great deal of paperwork to process now that he was in the country. He welcomed the news, and yet something in the way Mol hesitated made him uneasy.

"Then, when should I come in?" he asked.

"We'll hold an internal meeting to decide that."

Mol added that it shouldn't be more than a week to ten days. The man felt he ought to double-check what he had heard—the fact that he couldn't follow the language, even on the simplest of subjects, vexed him—so he echoed the words, "A week to ten days?"

"Nothing is confirmed yet," Mol responded. "It will depend on the outcome of the meeting."

Mol said that something had to be decided first among the managers. The man missed the first part of what Mol said, so he had no clue what exactly it was that had to be decided. He asked Mol to repeat it, but Mol told him he would call again after the meeting, assured him it would be held soon, and said they could discuss the matter then. Mol's response was so vague and open-ended that there was nothing for the man to repeat back to him.

He stalled for time, trying to drum up the words and sentences he needed in order to ask the things he wanted to ask and get the response he wanted to hear. But no matter how hard he tried, he realized that with his limited language abilities he had no choice but to leave it all to chance.

Mol must have felt more explanation was needed, because he added that the problem rested with Country C's peculiar situation. He said it would be a week at the latest until he could get back to the man with a decision. The man thought Mol said, "as long as there's nothing out of the ordinary," but he could just as easily have said, "as this is out of the ordinary."

He felt both relieved and anxious. The words, "at the latest," made him feel better. That meant nothing had changed about his work assignment. And if the words he had not quite caught at the end were indeed "as this is out of the ordinary," then that probably referred to him being asked to take a week to ten days off before starting work. "Country C's peculiar situation," on the other hand, made him uneasy. The country was facing both a garbage crisis and a spreading epidemic, and that would make it hard for anyone, even citizens, to feel at ease.

His curiosity left unsatisfied, the man exchanged several rounds of "thank you" and "sorry to inconvenience you," with Mol tacking on so many extra closing greetings that the man couldn't figure out when to hang up, before finally ending the call. As he was setting the phone back in its cradle, he realized he should have asked for Mol's phone number. He didn't even know his own phone number for the apartment.

He picked up the receiver and stared helplessly at it. The dial tone buzzed peacefully and evenly, not caring one bit that he didn't know the number. The tone was more or less the same as the dial tone back in his home country. But now that he could only receive calls and not reach out to anyone himself, the sound struck him as unfamiliar, and it finally sunk in that he was in a strange apartment in a foreign country.

Ever since he had been selected for the transfer to the head office—a temporary detachment that was to include management training—the deal had been on the verge of falling through. That had been the case up until the surprise email one week ago instructing him to leave the country. At first, his start date had merely been pushed back, and then, right around the time they started re-discussing the date of his transfer, the political situation in Country C went into abrupt turmoil. The long-reigning conservative party had been taking its power too far, and citizens were expected to rise up en masse. But in the end, there were only small, sporadic demonstrations that fizzled out as soon as they began. Elections took place despite the unrest, and the incumbent conservative party enjoyed an easy victory.

Then, when they were renegotiating his transfer date, rumors spread that a major earthquake was going to hit Country C. Located at the juncture of two tectonic plates, Country C was always on the verge of a quake, and geological societies around the world had predicted several different dates for a major one, based on certain warning signs. The dates of their predictions came and went without so much as a tremble, but the man's boss, the branch manager himself, prevented him from leaving because he had lost a cousin a few years earlier to an earthquake that struck the capital, right where the man was to be dispatched. If that one-in-a-million chance occurred and a dispatched employee was injured, the paperwork for processing his medical compensation would be very complicated indeed.

By the time his new transfer date was scheduled, the executives at the head office abroad had grown skeptical. Their concern was that it would be management training in name only, and that the real intention was to siphon off the head office's technology and expertise so the branch office could break away and go independent. Some were of the opinion that none of the branch employees were ready for a management position. The man's scheduled departure date grew closer and closer, but some of the executives remained unyielding in their opposition.

The only ones pushing for the transfer were the branch manager and a small handful of the manager's close associates at the head office, who had little say over the matter. While the final decision was being deferred, the man learned that the only reason the branch manager, who was close to retiring, had stubbornly insisted on naming a transfer employee despite opposition from the head office was so he could shore up his own position in the company. The man also learned that, despite his assurances that the transfer would happen, the branch manager lacked the power, drive, and necessary connections to realize his ambitions.

And so the transfer kept getting postponed, but this did not calm the ripples of discontent among his coworkers over the fact that the man had been selected for it in the first place. The most indignant was Trout—who had earned that nickname because his eyes were so wide-set that they made him look like a fish—and several coworkers who sided with Trout. Everyone felt that if anyone were to be made branch manager, it ought to be Trout, as he was the oldest and most experienced. They also thought that if anyone should be sent to the head office for management training, that person, too, should be Trout. Of course, even if seniority were not an issue and everyone had been hired at the same time, someone would still have to be promoted over the others, but they all felt the wrong man had been chosen.

His coworkers reacted poorly because they assumed the transfer meant something special. The first day the manager had arrived at the branch office, he had given a speech in which he categorically stated that the next branch manager would not be someone from the head office abroad. He also said that the next manager would have to work very closely with the head office, which meant work experience there would be an important factor, and that he was looking closely at potential transfer candidates. Everyone, especially Trout, took this to mean that the person who was transferred would be promoted to branch manager upon their return.

The man was just as much in the dark about why he had been chosen, so he pretended not to notice when his coworkers got together in the break room or around the water cooler to badmouth him or the branch manager for choosing him, or to criticize Mol, the human resources manager at the head office who had finalized the decision. Nevertheless, he was hurt that Trout, who had always been friendly and prone to pulling small pranks on him, suddenly turned frosty, and that his coworkers badmouthed him now with such fervor. Trout went around pretending to look sweet and innocent— with those fishlike eyes, all he had to do was open them wide—and did not hide the fact that he felt he was the victim of an unfair promotion. The employees spent every free moment at Trout's side, condemning the branch manager's biased decision and whispering about the man's lack of principles. But nobody bothered to ask the branch manager himself what the significance of the transfer was or why the man had been chosen for it.

"Rats."

When he was briefed on his transfer, the man had hesitated and then asked why he was chosen. That was what the branch manager told him.

"Rats?" the man asked.

"Yes, rats. As far as I can tell, no one is as fine a rat killer as you."

The branch manager's secretary giggled as she interpreted this for him. The man was crestfallen. There could not have been a more banal reason for him to be chosen for management training. Yes, they were a pesticide company, but wouldn't it have been better to say he showed great potential, or that he had an exemplary work attitude, or that his performance on the job was outstanding, or that he had a good head for business, or failing all of that, why not a little lip service from the manager saying that he simply liked him for no reason? Why, of all things, did it have to be because of filthy, disgusting, detestable rats?

"I'm sure I'm not the only one here who can kill a rat," the man said.

"Of course not. But other people would buy poison or set traps in the basement or what have you. I doubt any of them would try to kill a rat with their bare hands."

The man was still hoping to hear something nicer, but, for the manager, the case was open and shut: he had caught a rat.

His memorable encounter with the rat had occurred right after the manager's arrival at their branch. The manager had invited all of the employees to his housewarming. In the corner of the garden, a female coworker and the manager's preschool-aged son were enjoying a game of catch. The white ball looked so nice as it arced back and forth against the darkening sky that the man couldn't look away even while turning meat on the grill.

Just as everyone began tucking into the freshly grilled meat, the ball dropped out of the sky and rolled slowly across the mowed lawn. The woman and the manager's son turned to see where the ball went and gasped loudly. Past the end of the woman's stiffly pointing finger, back where the ball had rolled to a stop, was a large rat the size of a man's forearm, with fur as filthy as a rag used to clean a drain. The rat had stared, eyes round with fear, as the ball rolled menacingly toward it.

His female coworkers all shrieked, and everyone shouted at each other to kill the rat, that you needed poison to kill a rat, and why had no one thought to bring the branch manager some of the company's own rat poison, and they would be fine as long as it didn't come any closer, and maybe they should just let it go since they didn't have any poison anyway. They were used to handling live rats in the lab, and yet no one thought to simply kill it. After all, this was not one of the small, pink lab rats they were used to but an enormous, dirty, filthy sewer rat. The truth was that rats outside of a lab were terrifying.

The man was forced to get up and grab a purse on the chair next to him. It was the only thing handy that he could throw without breaking it or sending shards of glass across the lawn. He felt obligated to kill the rat because Trout was standing behind him, nudging him on. Of the male employees at the party, he was one of the more recent hires, and as this made him the most subordinate, he had no choice but to do something, with or without rat poison or rattrap. The rat, too, was clearly the runt of its litter. It was there, in unfamiliar territory, because it had been pushed out of the battle for food closer to its burrow. He and the rat faced each other silently, as if reading each other's troubled thoughts.

The moment he hurled the bag at the frightened rat, he heard one of the women scream. He thought it was because she was picturing the rat's splattered guts, but only after it left his hands did he realize the bag was hers. For better or worse, the bag landed squarely on top of the rat. He might have been imagining it, but the man thought he heard something burst. The sound of a water balloon popping echoed in his ears like a cassette tape playing the same section over and over. The sound did not stop until he heard the woman exclaim that she still had payments left on the designer bag.

"What a waste." Trout laughed at him as he stood there looking bewildered. "Why on earth did you grab *that* bag?"

"What do you mean?"

"You can tell by looking at it that it's expensive. You should've picked a cheap one."

"But that was the only thing handy . . ."

"Then throw the bag but miss the rat. That's what you should've done."

"What's the point of throwing something if you're going to miss on purpose?"

"It's just one little rat. Who cares if it gets away? What matters is that you stepped up." Trout lowered his voice. "All that matters is the branch manager saw you step up. That's all that ever matters. But squashing it to death? That's nasty. I can't stand nasty."

Trout was right about not throwing that particular bag at the rat. He could tell at once that the corner was dented in and the leather was scratched. He didn't have to look at the bottom of the bag to know there was blood, gray fur, burst rat guts, and lumps of pink flesh stuck to it. The contents were scattered across the lawn. He slowly picked up a pouch, a pencil case, and a small notebook. When he picked up a menstrual pad and saw the logo of a winged angel on the wrapper, an ill-timed laugh almost escaped him, but he heard the owner of the bag burst into tears. He could also hear the others muttering that they'd lost their appetite for barbecued meat and whispering, "What's he got in his hands now?" He would never laugh at an angel with wings again. Nor would he throw any more purses, and he would have to develop an eye for recognizing designer bags. But above all, he resolved never again to kill another rat. As he stepped forward to clean up the little corpse, his coworkers stepped back to avoid him. They acted like he was the rat. He had picked up the disgusting remains with the burst entrails dangling and carried them over to the trash can, and had vowed to himself that he would sooner be a rat than have to kill another.

"When I saw you grab that rat by the tail, with its intestines hanging out, and throw it in the trash, I was so moved," the manager said.

He didn't know whether to be modest and say it was nothing or to be bold and promise to kill any rat that appeared in the manager's garden, so he kept quiet and listened. The secretary pressed her lips together to keep from laughing. The man likewise found it hard to buy the idea that someone could be moved by the death of a rat. He was starting to see why his coworkers kept badmouthing him.

Thanks to the gossipy secretary, his coworkers found out that he had been selected for the transfer as a reward for the splattered rat, his horrible indifference toward his female coworker, and his ruining of a designer bag with payments still left on it, and they started calling him a lucky rat. They used it as further proof of how unfair his promotion was. Whenever he made even the slightest mistake at work, they spoke up in unison about his terrible job performance and criticized the manager for his biased handling of personnel. His coworkers were all too happy to point out his subpar language skills, his lack of leadership abilities, and the fact that he had accomplished absolutely nothing on the job that qualified him for the promotion.

It was true, every bit of it, but the manager only supported the man all the more, saying that leadership skills were a by-product of position and power, and that accomplishment was a by-product of doing one's job. In other words, once you had the position, you naturally became a leader, and if given the duties, the accomplishments followed. The manager even claimed that the man's poor language skills didn't matter. Being transferred did not mean you were immediately thrown into a work project, the manager said. The man would have several months to adapt, during which he could devote himself to language study. Just look at how much he'd grown in the few years since he started here, the manager added—though he did not specify in what ways the man had grown—and said he expected him to make great strides in his language acquisition as well.

The man's mastery of the language of Country C stopped at the basics. Right after he was chosen for the transfer, he had rushed through a three-month-long introductory class. But a long time had passed since then. The transfer itself was so uncertain that he couldn't justify spending more time on language study. Work was always busy, his coworkers who had more seniority were annoyed with him and kept dumping the kind of work on him that was tedious and time-consuming but would not yield any great accomplishments, and he had to work overtime almost every day. What was worse, his relationship with his wife had been turning sour, so he had no time at all to think about studying another language.

Since he had barely finished the introductory level, he could only express extremely simple emotions and childish, primitive desires. He could describe basic things, but he could not discuss anything concrete or weighty. He could convey what emotion he was feeling, assuming of course that it was relatively straightforward, but he could not explain how he came to feel that way. When he expressed his intentions or made requests, he did not know how to do so politely and so tended to use imperative sentences or direct orders. His language teacher evaluated him as sounding cold and authoritative.

The last grammar pattern he had learned in class was the causative-passive form. The pattern was unique to the language, and it implied a kind of forced complicity, being made to do something one did not want to do. He had learned it by memorizing the example sentence in his textbook: "Did you receive a summer vacation bonus from your company last month?" "No, I was let go." "I'm sorry. That is a shame." To put it in causative-passive terms, he was forced to repeat something he was loath to say over and over without end. By the time he had mastered the pattern, he felt as low as a worker who thought he was getting a bonus but got fired instead, and any time he found himself having to speak the language, the first words on the tip of his tongue were, "No, I was let go."

To make matters worse, he knew almost nothing about the cultural, social, or political situation there. He knew they used the same calendar as the rest of the world, along with their own traditional calendar based on the kings' reigns, but he did not know which year of whose reign it was. He knew the name of the current prime minister, but he kept forgetting the name of the conservative party to which the prime minister belonged and, though he remembered the names of several previous prime ministers, he could not name them in order.

The branch manager had noted his opinion of the man's foreign language learning ability at the bottom of the recommendation letter he sent to Mol, who would make the final decision. After receiving the letter, Mol had called the man directly and interviewed him over the phone, but Mol spoke so fast that it was nearly impossible for someone who had only passed an introductory class to understand him. The man tried to mimic the manager, who mitigated everything he said with "I think," so that no matter what Mol asked or requested of him, his responses sounded as cookie-cutter as a jobseeker out on his very first interview: "I have a lot to learn, but I think I will do my best."

To his coworkers, he was a complete disgrace. The coworkers who sat near him could hear him stammering awkwardly into the phone, but even the ones who sat farther away had all gathered behind him during the phone interview, just so they could eavesdrop and laugh at him.

At the end of the clumsy interview, he thanked Mol and said, "Sorry to trouble you." The moment he hung up, his coworkers surrounded him and said sarcastically, "Yeah, you should be sorry," and "If you know you're going to be sorry, then why say anything at all," and "You'll always be sorry. You're a disgrace to this office," before returning to their desks. He remained seated, enduring their sharp stares, and muttered to himself, "You're the ones who should be sorry." He squeezed the phone tight until his palms turned sweaty and he had to wipe them off on his pants.

Though the branch manager was the one who chose him for the transfer, his coworkers took it out on him instead. They continued to follow the manager's orders, laugh loudly at the manager's little jokes, and let him choose the restaurant whenever they went out for lunch together. The man, on the other hand, could not get any help from his coworkers while synthesizing and testing new pesticides, and he was left out of all company updates, shared meals, and even jokes. Long after the transfer had been continually postponed and seemed as if it were not going to happen at all, he still kept his distance from the break room whenever he saw two or more of his coworkers in there at the same time, and if someone else was at the vending machine when he went to get a cup of coffee, he would use the machine downstairs instead. He even stopped socializing with the other employees around his age who'd joined the company at the same time as him.

He knew the transfer was the only reason they tormented him. No one had thought ill of him before that. Up until he was selected, he was, like any other employee, close enough to some of his coworkers to exchange secrets with them, secrets that others in the office did not know—though most secrets ended up being leaked or revealed anyway. There was one colleague with whom he did not get along, yet during meetings they were in sync. He would present an idea, and that colleague would almost always second it. There was another employee too with whom he was not very close. Their desks were far apart, so other than a hello in the morning, they never spoke. But whenever they happened to be seated together, they greeted each other warmly and sounded genuinely regretful about being so distant with each other. In other words, when it came to both interpersonal relationships and office life, his were perfectly ordinary.

But now, for no other reason than that he'd been chosen for the transfer, he was bearing the brunt of his coworkers' jealousy. Ostracized by his coworkers, he couldn't get anyone to cooperate with him on the job, which only fulfilled their criticism of him: he never got to exhibit his leadership skills, and his job performance declined. The less likely it seemed he would ever be transferred, the more he longed to leave. He wanted to free himself of his coworkers, who were itching to stab him in the back. For someone like him, whose life was ordinary beyond compare with no more promise than a tiny, low-interest savings account, the transfer abroad was like an expensive insurance policy with a guaranteed payoff.

The glass doors that led out onto the balcony revealed a mosaic of lit and unlit windows in the apartments across the airshaft. The glow from the windows spilled into the dark and glimmered like stars against his balcony doors. He stared spellbound at it. As long as he looked only at those lights, as long as he did not think about the smell and the garbage that filled the streets, then this night was no different from those back home. At home, whenever the night felt too dark, all he had to do was look at the bright city lights, and when it got too quiet, he had only to listen to the rumbling of voices coming through the walls. Even with everything else here as hazy as a dream and as vague as a ghost, this night, this identical night, filled him with a sense of reality.

In front of the apartment building was a park, small enough that he could take in the whole thing in a single glance. It had two street lamps and a lighted telephone booth that kept the park illuminated despite the late hour. In the round lawn at the center, trees with wide trunks dangled their long branches in every direction. They looked like they would give good shade at midday. He noticed there were people sitting and lying on the park benches. They never budged, no matter how long he watched, so he figured they must be homeless. As he stared down from his window, a large bird, probably a crow, which had been clinging to a tree branch like black fruit, took to the sky and let out several strange cries. It was the first sound of a living thing he had heard in his new apartment.

To the right of the balcony door, a single-sized bed was covered in freshly laundered cotton sheets, and near the foot of the bed was a two-door built-in wardrobe. Lined up across from the bed were a television set, a small desk, and a chair. Two types of kitchen knives, bowls of various sizes, and a few spotless pots and pans were neatly arranged on the kitchen counter, and next to the kitchen sink was a separate laundry closet with a small twelve-pound-capacity washing machine. In the bathroom was a toilet and shower booth (so small that it looked like he would be slamming his elbows into the walls whenever he reached for the soap). That was the extent of his lodgings, but it was enough for him.

Once he had had a good look around the apartment, he decided to change into his pajamas, which were as familiar to him as his own skin, and realized that he'd left his suitcase in the hallway. He ran to the door. The hallway was empty. His suitcase was gone. The suitcase, so heavy that it had seemed to hold the entire world, had vanished. He stared in disbelief at the spot where had left it, at where he was certain he had set it down, but the hallway with its rough carpet was not saying a word. It was so quiet that it seemed there was nothing out there but darkness. The row of evenly spaced metal doors lining the hallway were firmly shut and looked as if they had never once been opened. He began to doubt himself. Maybe no one had snatched his bag, maybe he was mistaken in thinking he had left it out there in the first place.

The entry light shone down blankly on him as he scowled at the floor. He peered around at the dark hallway that had conspired in the loss of his suitcase and then walked to the left while scanning all eighteen of the apartments on the fourth floor. The motion detector lights mounted above each of the apartment numbers flicked on and off in turn as he passed them. He examined the bottoms of the doors closely to see if he could tell whether the occupants were awake, but not a single door had light leaking out from under it.

After reaching the end of the hallway and returning to his own apartment, the man warily scrutinized several of his neighbor's doors, each with a peephole set in the center like a single eye. The doors stared grimly back at him. During the brief time that he had been in his apartment, one of those doors had opened and someone had quietly sneaked out and carried his heavy suitcase inside. If they pulled it, he would have heard it dragging across the floor. It might have even left tracks in the carpet. Since there were no tracks and he had heard nothing, that meant they had to have picked it up, but the person would have to be big and strong to lift it so easily. That was the best he could infer from its disappearance.

He scanned the closed doors one by one and tried to remember what he had packed—other than the weight of the world, that is. He had packed hastily the morning of his departure, so he could not remember for certain what was in there, but he had definitely grabbed some clothes and under-wear. He must also have packed basic toiletries (though now he questioned whether he'd managed even that) and he recalled opening the shoe cabinet, which meant that he'd brought an extra pair of shoes. He had also stuffed in some CDs and DVDs that caught his eye, as well as a few books. The one fortunate thing was that the files he needed for the planning meeting were on his laptop, which he had brought in a separate bag along with a dictionary and his passport. The more he thought about it, the more he realized that he wasn't really attached to anything he had packed. The suitcase that had seemed to carry the weight of the world was really nothing more than a collection of insignificant objects, only so much dead weight. Not having clothes to change into right away was inconvenient, but at least the things he lost could be easily purchased in Country C. He regretted losing the books, as they were in his mother tongue, but he figured it wouldn't hurt to slowly read some books in the local language, for practice. As it turned out, none of the items that had weighed so heavily in his suitcase were irreplaceable. As long as he had the cash to buy them, that is.

He felt a little down, not solely because of the lost suitcase, but because of the whole string of unfortunate events that had plagued him since his arrival. But he comforted himself with the thought that everything that had happened would serve as a talisman against future mishaps during his stay, and that they would make for funny anecdotes later, just as the inspector at the airport had said. He had a tendency to feel defeated and lose courage whenever things didn't go his way, but he would dust himself off and pull himself together this time because he remembered that he had seen security cameras installed in all of the hallways when he first entered the building. He would ask the building superintendent for help, and once he'd had a look at the security tapes, he would find out who had taken his suitcase. Everything he thought he had lost would soon be returned to him. The worst thing he could do was jump to negative conclusions.

Pessimism was a self-fulfilling prophecy. That was his first thought when he went back inside and realized that his cell phone was gone too. He had turned it off and put it in the suitcase along with the charger. The only phone numbers he had brought with him were stored in the phone. Getting in touch with friends back home wouldn't be impossible, but it would require multiple, annoying rounds of long-distance calls. Not that he had any friends in particular that he spoke to regularly or made a point of touching base with. When he thought about how hard it would be to call anyone, he felt broken off from the rest of the world. If he failed to recover his phone, he would be cast out from the world of communication itself, just as his initial burst of pessimism had dictated.

He tried hard to suppress those thoughts and kept telling himself that all he had really lost were some clothes and electronics, all easily replaceable. The more he repeated this to himself, the more he missed his old pajamas, and the more he wanted to pick up the phone and talk to someone, anyone at all. He would never get to sleep now without those pajamas, no matter how tired he was, and he wouldn't be able to relax until he heard his mother tongue.

His throat was parched. The water was undrinkable. The tap must not have been used in a long time, as rusty water kept pouring out. He took a bowl from the cupboard and placed it under the faucet, which gushed and spurted like the pipes were going to burst, waited for the rust to settle, and then carefully sipped the clean layer of water on top. He'd never had to drink rusty water before, except for one time as a child when he and his friends were messing around, and he remembered how even then he had rushed to rinse his mouth out. Nevertheless, he drank it as easily as if he had always been drinking rusty water. He filled several bowls, but still the water came out mixed with rust, and his thirst did not go away though he drank until his stomach was full.

He lay on the bed, pulled the blanket up to his neck even though he wasn't cold, and turned on the television. His head ached each time he thought about all he had lost; he knew he would have to do something about it. Since it was the middle of the night, most of the channels had colorful test patterns. Only one was still broadcasting the news.

A reporter and a news anchor seated in a studio were having a heated exchange. The video footage they showed was as slow and choppy as a clip from an old movie. The quality was so bad that he guessed it had been filmed with a small handheld camera rather than a news camera.

The camera panned aimlessly across some houses, then a large hospital suddenly came up on the screen. Men dressed in the same hazmat suits as the health inspectors at the airport were loading a stretcher covered with a white cloth into an ambulance. The cloth hung limply. It reminded him of a white flag raised by enemy troops surrendering in battle. Whatever was on the stretcher looked more like a corpse than a patient—the cloth was pulled all the way up over its face.

Despite his attempts to focus on the news report, it kept getting interrupted by commercials. In contrast to the dismal and depressing news, the commercials were giddy and comical. Like premonitory symptoms of depression. Images of death were followed by a man seemingly excited to death by a swig of frothy beer. When the commercial ended, the screen changed back to the anchor grimly reporting the news, and after a moment, the exact same beer commercial came on again. The beer was called Zero and claimed to be the world's first completely nonalcoholic beer. The commercial paid no mind to the man's wondering why anyone would bother to drink a beer that would not get you drunk. Back and forth he went between the epochal-sounding birth announcement of a nonalcoholic beer and the doomsday-sounding news report of someone's death, before he finally, suddenly slipped into sleep.

THREE

The world beyond the front door was filled with white vapor. The clouds seemed to have lost their hold on the sky and fallen to earth. A musty, acrid scent wafted toward him, as if to tell him these were no clouds. As the smell spread, the vapor, which had started off as thick and puffy as a giant cotton ball, slowly began to unravel. The man stepped outside to see a sprayer truck with a fogging unit attached to the back going around the corner of the park in a cloud of chemicals.

He assumed the trash was the reason for fumigating. Not only were the streets littered, even the soil beneath the marble on which he stood was filled with garbage. The marble floor in the lobby gleamed. It looked like it was cleaned regularly. But when he thought about what lay beneath, he felt afraid. The earth threatened to rumble and rip open right beneath his feet.

HYE-YOUNG PYUN

He stared at the unraveling cloud of vapor and dove head-long into the center of it, just as he used to do when he was a child playing behind the trucks that sprayed for mosquitos. He would have chased after the truck too, if there had been at least one other person doing the same as him. The cloud thinned into a fine mist. The smell enveloped him. But the childhood memories conjured up by the smell were so banal that they made him more anxious than homesick. The disinfectant would not keep him safe from trash and disease; he could have doused himself from head to toe in its toxic brew and it still would not be enough to fend off the virus or keep that foul stench away from him.

The sprayer truck circled the block again. The building superintendent was still not there. The man's coughs came harder, probably brought on by the acrid chemical fog. He'd had a lot on his mind since his arrival, but the one thought that had stayed with him was the conviction that he had to hurry up and get over this cold. Growing impatient, he was about to leave, to look for a pharmacy instead, when a man dressed in a silver hazmat suit appeared. Half-hidden by the clouds of disinfectant, the man looked like a legless ghost.

As the hazmat suit headed toward the superintendent's office, the man shouted after him that he was the tenant who had moved into apartment number six on the fourth floor the night before. In his haste, he stumbled over his words. The hazmat suit sailed into the office, the door closing behind him, as if he had not heard him. Offended, the man went

42

back into the building and rapped hard on the black curtained window of the office. The superintendent pulled the curtain back, visibly reluctant, but did not open the window.

The man explained again that he was the new tenant. He raised his voice as he tried to tell the superintendent that he had set his suitcase down in the hallway the night before and, while his back was turned, someone had stolen it. But he wasn't sure how to say "while my back was turned," so he changed it to "after a while." He was nervous. If the superintendent got impatient, the curtain might close before he was done speaking, and this made him stutter even more.

The superintendent shook his head. He seemed to be saying he knew nothing about it. The man spoke more slowly, taking care not to get angry.

"I know that you don't know anything about it. But I think you should try to find out who took it."

He did his best to sound polite, though he frankly didn't understand why he should bother. The superintendent continued to shake his head and say nothing. The man pointed to the security camera installed in the ceiling to indicate that he wanted to check the footage from the night before.

"It's broken." At last, the superintendent spoke.

The man stared at the ceiling in disbelief.

"How long has it been broken?"

"Broken. It's broken."

As the man stood there staring at the ceiling with his eyebrows raised, he figured out why he felt so flustered and intimidated. The superintendent had a habit of scowling each time he said something, which made the man feel like he was being a pest and complaining for no reason.

The superintendent scowled again and rattled off a long sentence that the man could not even begin to grasp—the only word that stood out was "pharmacy." Was the superintendent saying that he'd just come from a pharmacy and that was why he hadn't been at his post during working hours? Or was he advising the man to go to a pharmacy? The superintendent repeated the sentence over and over and then shut the black curtain as if to say he had no further reason to continue talking. The man banged and banged on the door, but the curtain did not open a second time.

Thick clouds of pesticide flocked through the streets. The sharp smell of the chemicals stung the man's nose. But at least it was an improvement on the stink of garbage that had assaulted him the night before. His situation had not improved in the slightest, but the smell had.

When the chemical fog finally lifted, the trash-filled streets revealed themselves again. Maybe it was because of the trash, but there were almost no pedestrians on the sidewalks. The only people who caught his eye were police officers wearing hazmat suits over their uniforms. In fact, almost everyone he had seen so far wore one of the suits: the health inspectors and medical examiners, the superintendent, the police. He had no doubt it was due to the virus. Uncollected garbage could make people sick, but nobody would wear one of those suits just for that. Each time he saw someone wearing a protective suit or a dust mask, he worried that the virus might be spreading faster than he'd thought and he felt defenseless and afraid.

The roads, on the other hand, were badly congested. Most of the cars had only one person in them, and the few buses that he saw were empty, as if they were all simultaneously arriving at their terminus. Traffic was so snarled, rendering the traffic lights ineffective, that the sprayer trucks, which never ceased their assigned rounds, abandoned the jammed roads and drove on the sidewalks instead. Now and then, a car would follow a sprayer truck and drive shamelessly up onto the sidewalk too, but they were immediately pulled over by the police out on patrol. Police cars raced down the sidewalks in pursuit, sirens wailing, and forced the errant cars back onto the road. Driving on the sidewalk was hardly any faster though, as the drivers had to plow through mountains of refuse, trash flying out to the sides like it had been hit with a backhoe or exploding under the tires like firecrackers.

The sprayer trucks left behind a thin layer of powdery disinfectant that coated the sidewalks. The man's feet kicked up flurries of the stuff. He had no idea where to find a pharmacy. He had his mind on cold medicine, but what he really wanted was one of those puffy suits. He didn't know how effective they were at preventing infectious diseases, but to his eyes, they looked as good as armor.

He left the main street, which was backed up with cars, and ducked down a side street. It, too, was clogged with garbage, but there was much less car noise. He thought to himself it would be nice to find a place to eat, but nothing was open. There weren't even any other pedestrians whom he could ask about nearby restaurants. When he had made his way down several side streets and emerged onto another main road, he came across a small pharmacy. He nearly walked right by—it was tucked out of sight between two larger buildings. He ran toward it, narrowly avoiding a car that had just driven onto the sidewalk. Fortunately, the security gate was raised, which seemed to mean the pharmacy was open, though the lights were turned off inside.

As he drew closer, he saw that the plate glass window in front had been smashed. The little shop was in ruins, as if a massive earthquake had struck there, and only there, in the middle of the night. A flower planter out front had spilled its soil, and a fallen tree stretched its thick branches imploringly toward the door. The window display was empty. It looked like it had been given a violent shake: the drawers were hanging open, and empty medicine boxes were strewn across the floor. Shards of glass were everywhere, crackling underfoot with each step. A woman inside the pharmacy was sweeping broken glass into a dustpan. Judging by the easy way she moved inside the shop, which was still dark despite the morning light that found its way in, he assumed she was the pharmacist.

Though he knew he could just step inside, he stood clear
of the destroyed shop and called out to her that he was looking for cold medicine and a hazmat suit. She kept her eyes on
the broom and ignored him.

Just then, a large stone flew close to where he was standing and shattered what was left of the plate glass window.
Any closer and it would have hit him. The pharmacist ducked
behind the counter, looking shocked. As the man ran to put
distance between him and the building, he realized what
had happened: other people had been by earlier, putting
rocks through the window and ransacking the shelves. The
rock thrower stepped into the pharmacy carefully, to avoid
hurting himself on the long, uneven shards. His unusual air
of caution made him look like he was the one who had narrowly avoided being hit with a rock rather than the one who
had done the throwing. The man slowly crept back as the
pharmacist poked her head above the counter. He watched
as she stood face to face with the rock thrower, who glared at
her and loudly ordered her to do something, his face looking
anxious and hunted. He seemed exhausted, as if he had been
carrying that rock a long way, searching for something, or
looking for something to steal.

The pharmacist took it calmly. It was a shame, but she
seemed to know that the man was not there to hurt her and
that, despite the damage done to her pharmacy, there was
really no one whom she could blame. Her face was surprisingly serene. It might have been a look of resignation, but she

seemed at ease, perhaps because there was nothing left for her to protect. If you have nothing to lose, you have nothing to fear. Discouraged by the pharmacist's cool demeanor, the rock thrower gave a half-hearted glance around the store. Unless he needed cardboard boxes, there was nothing to take. He left, still empty-handed.

After the rock thrower left, the pharmacist came out from behind the counter, picked up the rock from the floor, and tossed it outside. The rock rolled weakly across the street and stopped against a black garbage bag. The pharmacist asked the man what he wanted. He knew from looking at the shelves that there was no point, as there was almost nothing left in the way of medicine, but he told her he was looking for cold pills and a hazmat suit, if only to give her an answer.

"I will pay you. I am not a thief," he said.

The pharmacist burst into laughter.

"That's a funny-sounding accent," she said. "I take it you're a foreigner? I could ask the same of you: Got any medicine I could buy?" She looked at him and laughed again. "You can see for yourself that I've got nothing. Someone already cleaned me out. They didn't even know what they were grabbing and took pesticides as well. But there is some bug spray and rat poison left."

She pointed at a chair behind the counter. He had trouble understanding what she'd said but he recognized the items under the chair from their labels.

"That's obviously not for colds," she added. "If you need it, you can have it. But I doubt you need it."

"My cough is severe. Is there nothing for it?"

"Drink lots of warm water. That's the best you can do."

The man started to leave, then stopped and asked, "May I take those?"

He had no particular plans in mind for the bug spray and rat poison. The rat poison could be useful for analyzing existing products on the market when he started working at the head office, but someone had probably already done that. As for bug spray, there was always a use. His apartment was probably crawling with insects from all of the neglected trash outside.

The pharmacist eyed him suspiciously. "That stuff won't help your cold. You understand? As long as you understand that, you can take it." She placed the bug spray and rat poison in a black plastic bag. "You said you're not a thief, so are you going to pay me?"

Flustered, he fumbled in his pockets for money.

"See, *now* you're a thief," she said jokingly.

The man drew his bruised hand across his throat like a knife and laughed.

As he left the pharmacy with the bug spray and rat poison, he figured that most of the stores had closed because they were worried that what happened to the pharmacy would also happen to them. He had unwittingly found himself in a place where you could not get medicine without resorting to robbery and where, for all he knew, everything else would have to be obtained the same way as well.

He wanted to rush back to his apartment, but he could not. The spray from the constantly circling trucks obscured the buildings and shops and kept the ground coated in a layer of powdery chemicals, making everything look alike. Even the piles of black garbage bags and homeless men picking through them looked identical. The more he wandered, the more the air filled with vapor, and the taller the piles of trash seemed to grow.

When he had exhausted himself with trying to find his way back, he flopped down onto one of the garbage bags. He knew it was trash, but it was the only thing there for him to rest against. As he breathed evenly, trying to adjust to the stench, he glimpsed a pair of legs coming toward him through a cloud of disinfectant left by a retreating truck. The legs drew closer. He stood up. He brushed the dirt off the back of his pants, but there was nothing he could do about the smell.

The legs belonged to a tall, thin man. His shirt and pants were neat and unwrinkled, as if they had been recently laundered and ironed. He stopped the tall stranger and asked for his help finding his address, but he could barely make out what the other man was mumbling from behind the dust mask he wore. He managed to catch a few directional words, like left, right, and across. He turned his back on the stranger, staring worriedly down the street he was being told to take, the street that was indistinguishable from all of the other streets behind their veil of litter and disinfectant, when something hit him on the head.

It wasn't enough to knock him out, but he lost his balance and fell into the pile of garbage. His head felt like it was on fire. He gingerly touched the back of his skull: the flesh there felt swollen and strange from the impact, as though a helmet had been slipped over him. His fingers were sticky, but he had no idea if it was blood or from something wet seeping out of the trash. Lying in the pile of garbage, he watched as the stranger who had struck him looked inside the black plastic bag he had been carrying. The items couldn't possibly be of use to the stranger. If it had been food or much-needed medicine, the man would have fought back, bleeding head or not. The stranger examined the bug spray and rat poison and tossed them away. As he hurriedly retreated, the stranger glanced back once at the man, not with a look of guilt but rather worry that the man might regain his strength, right himself, and come after him.

The man lay still among the garbage bags until the stranger's long, thin legs had vanished back into the chemical fog. If he could have stood up, he would have hit the stranger on the back of the head just to get even, but the pain kept him from rising.

After a while, he checked again to see if the bleeding had stopped, then picked himself up. Pain flared up his spine, and his body ached like an old woman's. The smell was worse than before. The foul garbage stench had mixed with the acrid disinfectant and was wafting off his battered and bruised body. While lying there, enduring the pain, he had become a part of the smell. He was no longer a newcomer to a foul-smelling world but was now of that world himself. He swallowed his nausea, as if to side with this part of him that assimilated so quickly to smells, and slowly walked away. There was no reason to rush; he had nothing to lose. The blow to the back of the head had told him that, here, problems were solved in a manner unlike anything he had experienced before; this was not a world where morals, order, education, and kindness were the norm, but rather one where plunder, pillage, violence, and garbage ruled. To survive in this world, he would have to be like that tall stranger. And if plundering and pillaging were a means of livelihood, then the only true asset was to own nothing.

The drone of the dial tone trailed from the receiver. The next time Mol called, he would have to get the phone number, but it would be another week to ten days before that would happen. He was idly listening to the dial tone buzzing in his ear when it finally hit him that all he had to do was call his office back home to get Mol's number. He couldn't believe it had only now occurred to him. It wasn't as if he were some mere tourist, he'd been sent there to work.

As he dialed the number of the company, he wondered if it was rude of him to try to call Mol. All he had were questions and favors to ask. He wanted to know if he could get health insurance benefits so he could see a doctor about his cold, and whether he could stay somewhere besides this garbage-strewn island. He had other questions too, like why on earth there was so much rotting garbage in the first place, why the pharmacy was robbed in the middle of the night, what the cause of death was for those bodies he saw on the news, whether he was correct in assuming the virus had killed them, why everyone insisted on driving alone and blocking up the streets, why he never saw anyone out walking, and why everyone he did see wore those ridiculous and uncomfortable hazmat suits, whether the epidemic really had gotten so bad that they had to wear them. But most of all, what he wanted to know was why he had been told, with no warning whatsoever, not to come into work for ten long days.

Just as the thought of all those questions began to be replaced by the worry that he would come off sounding like a big baby, someone answered the phone. It hadn't rung more than twice. The branch manager usually let two rings go by in order to warn whoever was calling that they were imposing on his time.

Trout answered. The man wished it were anyone else. When Trout asked who was calling, he blurted out, "It's me." It sounded like a confession.

"Well? Are you loving it over there at headquarters?" Trout asked as soon as he recognized the man's voice. He didn't bother to hide his sarcasm.

"Things aren't going well."

"Yeah, I figured as much. That's how things are all over the world lately, whether there's a recession or a boom. I mean, it's the same in this country too. Things aren't going well. But you already know that, don't you? Our idiot manager may be picky, neurotic, and stupid, but he's also a workaholic who loves to create more work for us. He let us have it again at the morning meeting today. Went on and on about virus this and personal hygiene that. What, are we seven-year-olds? My kid's already in the third grade, but I have to listen to the boss, who isn't that much older than me, lecture us every morning about washing our hands all the time and covering our mouths when we cough so our spit doesn't go all over the place. You know how he is. Oh . . . or maybe you don't. He always treated you special." Trout lowered his voice. "Hey, did you know? Yesterday, I went to get some papers signed by the manager, and I heard the funniest thing from his secretary. You know that email that came for you, the one with the start date of your transfer? Do you remember who sent it?"

He remembered clearly. It was Mol. The email contained a few formal remarks, briefly stated the conditions of the job, and noted that his start date would commence one week from the date it was sent. Trout didn't wait for him to respond.

"According to what I heard yesterday, they can't figure out who sent that email. I heard the branch manager talking on the phone with the supervisor at the head office and, what's that person's name again? It's something real common, but now I can't remember. Anyway, the supervisor said he never sent that email. They seem to think there was a computer problem at the main office. They said that all of the emails in the drafts folder got sent out at once. I have no idea if it's true, but it sounds like they've been busting a nut trying to undo the damage. The supervisor and branch manager are really upset about it. They've been making calls all over the place to find out if it was a mistake or not. I didn't get to hear the rest because someone came in just then, but it got me worried that maybe something had gone wrong with your transfer. So I called a few other people over at the head office, and what I gather is that *no one* there seems to know anything about your transfer. And they're the people you're supposed to be working with! So, anyway, I hear you got a ten-day leave of absence? That's what the branch manager said at the morning meeting. Figures you would get vacation over there when you did nothing here to deserve it."

"Some vacation. Everyone is in a state of panic over here."

"Panic? Ha! So are we. A state of panic. Everyone keeps asking why the hell you were picked. They keep grumbling about how you have no talent or experience. When you consider our disappointment, you could say we're pretty panicked, too."

"That's not what I meant. I mean, I don't know for sure, but it seems like everyone is panicking over the virus." His voice was strained from trying to suppress his anger.

"You mean that thing that's been going around? Don't worry. You know you're lucky. Nothing bad will ever happen to *you*, no matter what it is. Anyway, they say the fatality rate is low, so what are you so scared—"

He hung up on him. Trout probably had more sly jabs to make, but he didn't want to hear them. If the situation over here had not yet made the international news, and frankly even if it had, Trout could not possibly understand how desperate the man was feeling. Knowing Trout, even if he had seen the news, he probably laughed at the situation the man was in and reveled in it. He pictured Trout delighting in his failure and realized that he had no choice but to endure the situation.

He opened the balcony door. He had always been in the habit of standing in front of windows when he felt down. But the view of the city from his balcony did little to comfort him. The people passing by on the street were mostly dressed in protective suits and wearing dust masks. From time to time, he noticed people who were not wearing the suits, but the tattered condition of their clothing suggested they were homeless. In fact, there were several vagrants sprawled out like insects on the benches in the park.

Each time a sprayer truck made its periodic rounds, he burst into violent, consumptive coughing fits. The stronger the fog, the more often he coughed, but he had no idea whether this was the fault of the disinfectant, or whether it was because his cold had not gotten better, or whether he was perhaps now infected with the virus. At that thought, he took a deep breath of the disinfectant as it issued from a truck. He had to breathe in the stink of garbage at the same time, but it was better than being exposed to the virus. No one yet knew how it was spreading, and whether it had originally come from a dog or a pig or a cow or a rhesus monkey or a goat, and if so how it had then made its way into a human body. The only thing they did know was that there was no cure. The chemicals made his whole body itch. Though they weren't sprayed directly into his room, the walls and curtains were already beginning to stain. At this rate, even if he never became infected, he would probably die of chemical overdose. His bruises paled in comparison to the bright red sores that had opened up on his forearms.

As he stood there looking out, a line of legs moving at matching angles appeared through the cloud of disinfectant. Gradually, the cloud dispersed to reveal an army of police officers with hazmat suits over their uniforms. The officers broke off into smaller groups, each of which headed to a different building. One of the squads formed a line in front of his apartment building, each officer standing as straight and even as eggs in a carton. At the sound of a loud siren, they broke formation and swarmed inside.

The man cowered for no reason, and his heart began to race at some unknowable fear. The police must have been hunting down the suspect of a violent crime, and it must have been something pretty bad for them to mobilize so many men. After a moment, an announcement came over the loudspeakers installed inside the building. As the announcement repeated itself, he copied down the sounds of the words that he couldn't understand and looked them up in his electronic dictionary: *contagion, inspection,* and *quarantine.* Assuming he had pieced the words together correctly, the announcement meant that someone in this building or neighborhood was infected, and until all of the occupants had been inspected and found healthy, they were being quarantined in their apartments for fear of spreading the contagion.

FOUR

Meals were distributed at set times. It was not what he had pictured: people standing in long lines, waiting to receive rations from someone in uniform. Doing it that way would have meant bringing residents into contact with each other and defeating the purpose of the quarantine. Instead, police officers set plastic bags of food in front of each door, and those inside collected them after the officers had left. Each bag contained a boxed meal or a sandwich, plain water or a beverage. He did not care for the fact that the food was always the same, but at least it tasted better than expected.

After the food was set in place, the fire alarm was rung. The first time, they had not used the alarm, and a few people had opened their doors too late; their rations had been stolen. But the police couldn't search every apartment in search of a food thief when they did not yet know who was infected. They'd come up with the idea of using the fire alarm in a last-ditch attempt to remedy the problem. At the sound of the bell, everyone opened their door and retrieved their food in unison. There were no more complaints about stolen food.

Each time the bell rang, the man felt an uncontrollable urge to run. He thought he smelled something burning. But even if he hadn't imagined the smell of smoke, the alarm was still a constant reminder that he was locked in an apartment in a foreign country, that the building was teeming with the infected, and that he was, literally, in a state of emergency.

The eighteen doors on the fourth floor all cracked open in unison, the occupants already crouching down low like dogs or cats to grab the food from the ground as fast as they could. The man watched unhappily as his neighbors' hands reached out to snatch the bags, the doors slamming shut behind them, as if to keep any bad air out. They were not neighbors. They were thieves who had stolen his suitcase, and before long they would be looters who would not hesitate to steal his bread.

He was opening his door to retrieve his breakfast when he heard a dog bark from behind one of the other open doors. The sound jogged his memory loose. Flustered, he dropped the bag. He had left his dog behind. He remembered now. But what worried him was not the thought of his poor dog locked inside his apartment, whining with hunger for the last few days, nor was it the thought of what the woman next door might say (she couldn't bear the sound of barking and complained every time they crossed paths in the elevator that it woke her newborn baby and insisted he get the dog's vocal cords removed); rather, it was the realization that by leaving his dog alone in an empty apartment, he had failed in his responsibility to the dog, and he despaired at the thought that failure, for him, was only a matter of time. He told himself that he deserved to be living this way now, surviving on handouts like a dog. Indeed, the fact that he had not even thought about his dog for several days showed that he was lower than a dog.

In truth, he was not fond of dogs. To be precise, what he felt was closer to hatred. He had been taking care of the dog ever since he and his ex-wife split up, but he hated the way the dog would suddenly start barking for no discernible reason. Each time that happened, he thought of the saying that dogs could see ghosts, and a shiver ran through him. He hated the dog hair that clung to his suit jackets, even ones fresh from the cleaners, and he hated it when the dog rubbed against his legs and whined. He hated having to rush every morning to fill the dog's bowl with enough food for the day when he was already pressed for time, or how the dog would follow him to the front door and rub against his legs again, getting hair on his trousers, and he hated having to spend more time removing that hair. When he returned home from work, he hated having to pick up the dog's feces from the bathroom floor, and he hated it when he had to use the toilet himself before he had a chance to clean up after the dog. More than once, he had wanted to get rid of the dog, but each time, the thought of his ex-wife made him put up with it a little longer. Given all of that, he felt bewildered by his own excess of guilt.

The dog was as stupid as a dog can be, and yet it looked at him sometimes as if it knew everything, and when there was nothing to be afraid of, it barked ferociously and strutted around, but when faced with a threat, it tucked its tail between its legs and cowered and lowered its head. It whined to be taken out, and when he did take it on the occasional walk, it wore him out with its excitement, dragging him around as if he were the one leashed. In other words, it was a typical dog.

The reason he'd kept a dog that he hated was entirely the fault of his ex-wife. She loved the dog and had promised to take it after the divorce, but he stubbornly insisted on keeping the dog simply to prevent her from having it.

"Why do you keep asking for the dog?" he asked. "Don't you know how much I care about it?"

"I didn't know."

He felt a little guilty but didn't let that stop him.

"Well, now you know."

"I don't want to know," she hissed and hung up.

They repeated this routine at least seven times. Then, just when he had figured he'd gone far enough and decided to give her back the dog, she told him she could no longer look after it. He found out later that his ex-wife was already hot and heavy with Yujin by then, and Yujin hated dogs, too.

The man could no longer stand the dog and was impatient to return it to her, but she stubbornly refused. He threatened to abandon the dog, but she was undaunted and told him to go ahead. She was so intent on making the most of her second marriage that she refused him even the slightest consideration. It was only natural, but it made him nearly crazy with hurt. He felt like he was the one abandoned, not the dog.

But leaving the dog behind wasn't that big of a deal. At first it had him so flustered that he could barely think straight, but really all he had to do was call someone back home and ask them to get the dog—once he figured out who to call. Since his apartment had keyless locks, anyone could get in as long as he told them the passcode. He was hoping that whoever he managed to talk into getting the dog would also look after it for him, but if they couldn't, since looking after someone else's dog nowadays was no easy task, they could board the dog at a kennel instead or contact his ex-wife so she could take it. The dog would only have to go without food for one or two more days at the most until he could get in touch with someone. A couple more days wouldn't kill it.

He took the sandwich from the fallen bag and chewed it slowly, then suddenly remembered something else. The day he left the country, the dog had not followed him to the door. Usually the dog was so insistent, getting fur all over his pants every single time he left for work, that he had to kick the dog away just to squeeze through the door. But why, on that day, was it not by his side?

He had not packed until the morning of his departure. He should have started packing several days in advance or, at the very least, the day before, but the notice of his start date came as a surprise, and the closer the date came, the more he had to do, the more people he had to meet, and the more official and personal business he had to take care of. That was why he had not boarded the dog.

His old college friends had held a going-away party for him the night before he left. Or rather, they'd slapped that label on it at the last minute, but it was really just one of their regular get-togethers. Considering that he was leaving the next morning and hadn't even packed yet, he should have skipped it. But the friend in charge of organizing it pressured him to at least drop by, if only for a moment. The man knew the real reason his friend was so insistent was that it was his first time organizing one of their get-togethers, and having everyone there would be a big coup, but the man went anyway, intending only to eat dinner and leave. His transfer—everything about which, except for the start date, was now up in the air—had been intended to last a minimum of six months, but the transfer letter specified that if his work did not see results in that time, it could take as long as five years. For him as a single man, there was no difference between six months and five years spent abroad, so he didn't mind that his return date was unspecified. In fact, if he could have, he would have left sooner and stayed that much longer.

In the end, he did not leave the party early. Just as he was about to get up and go, Yujin walked in. Yujin was the real reason he'd joined them in the first place. Yujin exchanged a noisy round of greetings with everyone and took a seat near the door. Soyo, who was seated next to the man, started whispering to him.

"Did you hear? He got a divorce."

The man was shocked to hear this. Yujin had been married for less than two years, and to none other than the man's own ex-wife. If Yujin was divorced, then that meant his ex-wife was also a divorcée again. But she hadn't said a word about it to him.

Yujin, who was seated far away from the man, looked glum all throughout the party. But according to Soyo, it was not because of the divorce. Yujin was already involved with another woman. The man was amazed that anyone could go from marriage and divorce to a new love affair so quickly. He pitied Yujin's poor judgment and lack of success. That pity filled him with a pleasant sense of security.

As the rounds of drinks kept coming, some of the guys changed seats, some went home early, and others wound up slumped in corners, too drunk to move, and the man found himself seated next to Yujin. He affected a voice excited with drink and asked Yujin, who had so far pretended to ignore him, what secret power he had that enabled him to fall so tenaciously in love. Yujin could tell he was being sarcastic and said firmly that if he was talking about their ex-wife then he had nothing to say to him. The man wasn't interested in talking to Yujin about their ex-wife either. Especially not in a place like this, where their friends were paying close attention, eyeing the two of them seated side by side while pretending to stuff grilled meat in their mouths or tip back glasses of alcohol, like eyewitnesses to a scandal. But he could do nothing to prevent their curiosity.

"Zees woman, she ees terribly attractive, no?" one of their friends asked in a fake foreign accent, pretending to be drunker than he really was.

The man did not respond, but Yujin glared at the friend.

"Shut up."

"If she's not attractive, then what is she? Easy? Because otherwise, divorced twice—"

The friend didn't get the chance to finish. His mouth was closed for him by Yujin's fist. The man felt grateful to Yujin. It had been a long time since he had been able to take that sort of thing as a joke. The fun was instantly ruined, but in an effort to prevent a bigger fight from breaking out, everyone acted as if the friend had had it coming. The friend wrapped his hand around his throbbing chin and cussed at Yujin in a low voice while several other men held him back.

Yujin shook off the men who were trying to stop him and stood up. The friend looked like he was debating whether it would be better to hit Yujin back and recover some of his dignity, or to just take it and pretend to be the good guy. Nobody wanted the fight to escalate—not even the one who got punched wanted the evening to end in a pointless bar brawl—but he continued to glare stubbornly at Yujin, as if not doing anything would mean acknowledging that he was in the wrong and thus risking a wound to his pride.

Soyo, who had been nervously watching the two of them, jumped in and said, "The world is full of available women and everybody cheats, so why make such a big deal over divorce? Besides, it's not unusual for two men to love the same woman or for one woman to be in love with two different men, so why is it so scandalous for a woman to love two different men in a row?"

Soyo spoke eloquently on their behalf. But he and Yujin were offended all the same. They felt more deeply insulted than when their ex-wife was thoughtlessly called "easy," since Soyo seemed to imply that they were both fools who'd been played by the same woman. But to put a finer point on it, Soyo was not exactly right when he said that she'd loved them "in a row." Granted, their marriage was already on the rocks by then, but it was apparent that she had started seeing Yujin while she was still married to him. And she had continued to see him every now and then after she was married to Yujin.

No sooner had Soyo finished his long speech than the man's fist and Yujin's body both came flying at him. Soyo ducked the punch but was knocked backward onto the table with Yujin wrapped around him. Soyo grabbed Yujin's necktie and pulled. Yujin spluttered and choked. The others were barely able to pull them apart. When Soyo righted himself, blood was pouring down his face from a broken nose or a busted head or a split lip, or possibly all three at once. The man reached out to try to help clean up the blood, but Soyo shoved his hand away angrily.

"You're the bigger asshole. You two are exactly alike."

The man took Soyo's verbal abuse and then got up and followed Yujin, who'd already left to go to another bar.

To him, his ex-wife was not easy, she was incomprehensible. The manager of a piano school, she used to close up early and go out drinking with friends, and would call him at the last minute, no advance warning whatsoever, to inform him that she was spending the night at her friend's house. She would disappear for days at a time to take trips with friends, all of whom he knew only by their first names and nothing else. More than once he'd come home early from work and was resting when students' parents rang their home number to complain that the school doors were locked and the teacher wasn't answering their calls. Sometimes, just to get them off the phone, he lied and told them he was only a tenant. It was the same with family events that he absolutely had to attend. She would refuse to go if her feelings had been hurt or if she was simply not in the mood, and he would be hard-pressed to come up with excuses for her absence.

He overlooked her drinking and her frequent outings, her staying out overnight and taking off on trips, her neglecting the housework. He never felt he could express his anger by shouting at her, but she mistook his silence for understanding. Sometimes, out of the blue, she would give him an apologetic look and thank him, and each time she did this, his feelings were hurt and he had to admit to himself that he did not understand his wife in the slightest. He wanted other people to think he was a generous and thoughtful husband, and he did not want to scream and yell, so he did his best to tolerate the unacceptable. But, for the usual old-fashioned and conservative reasons, he secretly branded all of his wife's friends as trash and was deeply suspicious of whether she was faithful to him.

Whenever his wife was out of the house, he went through her desk drawers, examined one by one everything she wrote in her journal, and memorized all of the names that he found there. He painstakingly pondered the trivial contents of the notes she had written, interpreting lines of poetry that she had clearly jotted down for no reason, like "I'll have to pay for myself / with myself, / give up my life for my life," as metaphors for her infidelity, which left him simultaneously elated at thinking he'd found evidence and clutching at his aching heart as if he had caught her in the very act, only to wonder the next moment what on earth giving up your life for your life meant and concluding that his wife must have decided to live life a little more fully and nothing more. With that thought, he would feel relieved that his wife had not in fact cheated on him, while still despairing over the lingering suspicion that she had erased the evidence of some regretted indiscretion.

She was the first to suggest divorce. He raped her late one night, after she arrived home drunk from one of her outings. They'd already been headed for a split, but after that there was no going back. He had rolled off of her like trash succumbing to gravity, and she, still fully cognizant despite being drunk, got up from the bed, pulled her clothes back on, and in a cold voice told him that while adultery was forgivable, rape was not. Then she took her suitcase out of the closet and started to pack. Without bothering to pull his pants back up, he looked down at his flaccid penis and turned to lie facedown on the bed, stretching his limbs in an attempt to mimic the way their dog would stretch at their feet. Only then did he realize that he had done something he could never take back, and he lost the confidence to look his wife in the face. She sat with her back stubbornly turned to him as she packed her clothes. Bent over, her back with its prominent vertebrae looked thin and frail. He was overcome by an ill-timed urge to stroke the gentle curve of her spine (he reached his hand through the air toward her in vain) and wondered, if she really was walking out on him, where on earth was she planning to go, when would she be back to get her belongings that didn't fit in the suitcase, and was she only pretending to pack in order to give him time to apologize? When he observed how calmly she was packing, he began to suspect that she had anticipated this would happen and had been plotting all along to trick him into raping her so she could turn him into the guilty partner and divorce him. The more he thought about it, the more convinced he became that her emotional and psychological freedom, to say nothing of her sexual freedom, was more than he could handle. His only evidence of this was the unhappiness he felt over his wife's infidelity and the suspicion that had given rise to that unhappiness. He had questions, but she would refuse him any answers, and because he could not answer his questions himself, he kept his mouth shut. Even as he held back his words, he got the feeling it was not him but his wife who was holding back, and as he watched his wife's back bob up and down calmly, with no regard for his agitation or his suspicions, he realized that their marriage was well and truly over, even without his resorting to rape or the suitcase packed tight with clothes.

One night after the divorce, when he was alone in bed and masturbating, unable to ignore the urge, he tried to recall the sounds his ex-wife used to make in bed. It wasn't so much that he lusted for her as that she was the one he had slept with regularly, and though their sex life had not been all that great, he knew where she liked to be touched. He started imagining his ex-wife's stifled gasps only to burst out laughing and lose his erection. He realized he had confused her with an actress in a porn video he'd watched late one night when he had no other way of relieving the tension that flooded his hips. The only sound he clearly remembered his wife making in bed, if by that he meant any sound in bed at all, were the words, "You son of a bitch, we're through." Those were the words he heard the moment he violently shoved his erect self into her dry vagina. He'd heard those words and fucked her even harder, as though he really were a dog, but he had derived no pleasure from the deed, and he was left afterward with a deeper grief than he had first anticipated.

A few days later, as he was signing every page of the divorce papers his wife sent him, he felt lighthearted. Mere papers could not contain everything he had put up with, all of his suspicions, the things he'd thought he understood but didn't, and the things he might have actually understood to some extent but, by the time the ink was dry, he no longer cared about. The divorce went according to form, succinct and perfunctory, and required only their time.

From that point on, his suspicions regarding his wife's infidelity were left as neurotic misgivings. It was better for him to drop it, both for her sake and his. It was a good thing that he hadn't taken his suspicions any further. Who knew what he would have done if he had confirmed her infidelity? He had even seen a psychiatrist about it but still found it difficult to admit that unjustified doubts had taken over his mind. He wanted proof, and was willing to hire a detective if it came to that. For his sake, his wife *had* to have been cheating. He could not accept the idea that his marriage had fallen apart and that he had caused pain to the person he loved—in other words, that he alone had ruined everything—because of a mistaken idea. What drove him to that failure had to be something outside of himself, if not his wife's infidelity then a society that had driven him to suspicion.

Perhaps because he did not try very hard to hide the fact of his divorce, word got out on its own. Concerned that keeping silent in the face of people's curiosity would only inspire more lurid imaginings, he told people that his ex-wife had never once served him a home-cooked meal. It was too simple a reason for a relationship to end, and yet the people he talked to acted as if they now understood what kind of a wife she had been. His lazy excuse became proof that she had never loved him from the start. But he remembered that his ex-wife, who had neither an interest in nor a talent for cooking, had made stew for him several times, stew that came out tasting different each time she made it, and she had also on several other occasions served him some simple dishes. Had he eaten at home more often, she no doubt would have cooked more. Though her efforts were inconsistent, she did try to keep him healthy by grating mountain yam and mixing it with milk or boiling down red ginseng for him, and whenever he had a cough, instead of cough medicine, she gave him an herbal tonic made with balloon flower. He hated all of it and refused it each time, but secretly, it made him happy, and the idea of growing old together and putting each other's health first gave him a supremely warm feeling.

Truth be told, he had never had any real complaints about his wife's lack of interest in housekeeping, whether while they were legally married or after their marital relations were severed. He'd never actually bothered to sit down for a proper meal at home. Before and after he was married, he ate his breakfasts every morning in the company cafeteria. It was an old habit. The company started its workday earlier than others, and the only way he could have eaten at home and still made it to work on time was if he slept less. He always chose more sleep.

He was far from the only employee who ate breakfast in the company cafeteria. The facilities were nice, the cost was low, and the food tasted good. At lunchtime as well, he alternated between eating in the cafeteria and eating out at one of the restaurants near the office. On afternoons when he worked away from his office, he had dinner wherever he happened to be. Since he went into work most Saturdays as well, his meals followed the same pattern as on weekdays. The only time his wife could have served him a warm meal was on Sundays. But they usually spent their Sunday afternoons relaxing at home together or going out to the movies or for a walk in a nearby park. Sunday nights, then, found them preferring to eat out.

It was childish of him to blame her for the divorce, and it left him feeling more ashamed than when he had realized that he'd raped her. And yet, he blamed her anyway because he could not understand how things had reached that point. The worst had come to pass, but he understood none of it. It was hard enough to grasp how two people could start off as distant strangers to each other only to grow close enough to marry, so of course he could not explain why his marriage had ended. He had heard once that the farther away a galaxy is, the farther and faster it is moving from you. Perhaps it was the same with relationships. But there had to be some reason other than growing apart. He knew that much, anyway.

After the divorce was finalized, whenever he found himself alone with nothing else to occupy his thoughts, he would be overcome with longing to talk to his wife again. They had never talked about anything very important; most of it was so trivial that he couldn't keep track of whether something they'd talked about had happened that day or the day before. For example, there was the time a salesman got past the security guard at work and tried to sell everyone knife sharpeners. "Even with all that technology, a peddler still got into the building? Where was the guard? How did he get through the security system?" "It's been out of order lately." "Seems like everywhere you go, things are out of order." "You can get in anywhere as long as you know how to." The conversation continued as they were reminded of more things, and soon

they were marveling over the fact that peddlers had pro-
gressed from hawking knife sharpeners on the subway to
going into people's offices, and their meaningless comments
followed one after the other, as if worried they might run out
of things to say: "What are they selling on the subways nowadays?" "One guy was selling an iron-on patch for mending
holes in your stockings." "You should have bought one." He
told her that he had wanted to buy a knife sharpener, but
Trout bawled him out and ordered him to call security. Then,
when the peddler was dragged out of the office between two
security guards like a common thief, he had quietly stood up
from his desk, intending to follow them, but Trout was
watching, so he pretended he had to go to the bathroom
instead, though he really didn't. Their conversations had
nothing to do with their lives, and their lives never changed
as a result of those conversations, nor would they have
changed if they had not had them, and anyone listening
would have thought them fools to get so excited over topics
so trivial.

But he and his ex-wife knew that there was more to talking
than just sharing their future dreams, the impossibility of
ever realizing those dreams, and the faith that it would all
come true somehow anyway. Talking about their pasts
instead—about embarrassments and longings, about the
things they wanted back and the things they did not—was a
way to express regret for the times when their lives had not
overlapped, and to gladly serve as witness to each other's

lives. They participated happily in a present that was bound to vanish from memory because it was trivial and insignificant. And they did speak, despite themselves, of hope and determination, of the will to put the same into action, and of broken wills, and when they did, they gave each other words of unexaggerated encouragement, heartfelt consolation, and simple cheer.

He had not raped his wife out of hatred or some renewed surge of lust, he did it because he lacked the confidence to talk to her the way they once had and so he chose a foolish approach instead. Shortly before the divorce, they had taken an expensive and much-anticipated trip together, but even then he had been unable to talk to her and wound up returning home alone with only injuries to show for it. It made him lonely to realize that he had no one to listen to him and no one for him to listen to, but he did nothing to overcome his loneliness. He did not have any friends whom he could call up and have a long conversation with, and whenever he did meet someone, all they did was drink and bitch about life. He didn't want that.

When Soyo had told him about his ex-wife getting remarried to Yujin not long after their divorce, he had felt shocked and hurt. His first thought was that he would no longer get to lay in bed with his ex-wife, their heads resting on each other's bodies, as they passed the time chatting or retelling old stories that popped into their heads for no reason, stories that had already been told multiple times and had nothing new to offer. Those moments were among his favorites. He felt like crying when he realized that those moments were gone for good, but he didn't want to reveal any of this to Soyo, so he had hidden his reaction behind the rim of his beer glass, which had turned as lukewarm as his tears.

It was disappointing that his wife's taste in men was so bad that she had stooped to marrying someone like Yujin. Of course, he should have known her standards weren't that high, since she had also married him. He was not fond of Yujin. In fact, he sort of hated him. In his opinion, Yujin talked too much, exaggerated about his work, and pretended to be friendly and impartial until he sensed a disadvantage to himself, upon which he would turn mean and violent, brag that he was doing extremely important work, and flaunt his connections. He couldn't stand men like Yujin, so he would criticize Yujin's pretentious way of speaking and question the absurd things he said, only to be attacked for being too narrow-minded.

His ex-wife probably thought Yujin was charming—all the more so if she had tired of her ex-husband's own wishy-washy, introverted, insecure, and passive ways. Despite her tendency to do whatever she felt like, his ex-wife was timid and lacked confidence, and therefore did not reveal her feelings to other people easily. No matter how long you had known her, the moment she thought you were not on her side, she would clam up and respond defensively in order to protect her dignity, and then do something she regretted. To get her to open up, you had to take your time and listen to what she had to say, always be the one to start the conversation, and never rush her. Did Yujin really have that much patience? He pictured Yujin demanding to know why she was so quiet all the time, or responding with sarcasm or nagging her instead, but of course this imaginary version of Yujin had more to do with his desire for them to have problems and less to do with Yujin's actual personality.

His ex-wife had probably listened to Yujin's constant chatter and inability to hold his silence and thought it meant she knew him, then mistook knowing him for loving him and decided to get married again. She was a warmhearted person and bonded easily, or so he thought, and would open her heart in an instant to anyone who was friendly to her, and when that someone was of the opposite sex, mistaking simple openness for love was all too easy. That clearly must have been the case in her relationship with Yujin. Of course, he realized too late that it had probably also been the case in their own relationship.

That night, after leaving the party, he found himself drinking alone with Yujin. He worried about the packing he still had to do, but once it was just the two of them, they had nothing to say to each other and he was in no mood to talk anyway, so he figured the best thing to do was to get drunk quickly and use that as his excuse to hurry home. It was the only way to avoid the awkwardness.

He drank far more than usual but couldn't seem to get intoxicated, and the more shots he took, the fuzzier Yujin's face became until his ex-wife's began to appear in its place. He didn't like that. How could two faces that didn't resemble each other in the slightest overlap? He felt repulsed, as if he'd caught a glimpse of them in bed together, and he kept downing more shots.

He did not ask Yujin why they divorced. Just as he had unilaterally denounced his ex-wife to other people by saying that she had never once made him a home-cooked meal, Yujin as well might have made excuses about food, her spendthrift ways, or her habit of coming home late and sometimes staying out all night. To truly understand Yujin and his ex-wife, he would have to start by listening to the story of when they dated, followed by every last detail of their married life, and he absolutely did not want to hear that.

Yujin asked him something, and he reluctantly answered. The drunker the man got, the more his defenses came down, and soon they were answering each other's questions, sharing complaints, offering agreement, and laughing at themselves. Though he could not remember most of what he and Yujin talked about, the one thing he did remember vividly was when Yujin asked whether he knew that his ex-wife had cheated on him with Yujin when they were still married. It was more statement than question. He'd already guessed as much and felt hurt but was reluctant to let Yujin know that he felt hurt, so he swallowed hard and said that he knew she had been sleeping with someone but did not know it was Yujin, and that if he had known at the time, he would not have stood for it. Yujin stared him straight in the face and retorted that he understood exactly what he meant. The man didn't want to know what Yujin was thinking, so he said nothing and tried hard to avoid Yujin's sharpened gaze.

Had they still been married, he would have ignored the fact that he was in no position to criticize her. He might have pressed her for an explanation, got angry, shouted at her, and then, unable to control his anger, beat her or done something even worse. He knew he was capable of hurting another person when he was angry, even if it meant risking injury to himself. And just because they were divorced now, it didn't mean he could contain his anger.

But when he thought about his ex-wife, he missed her terribly. He was furious that she had abandoned and betrayed both him and Yujin, but he pitied her at the same time. And yet despite that pity, he felt no pangs, no torment, and he realized at once that his sympathy for her was greatly exaggerated. What truly broke his heart was not his ex-wife's life but his own, made all the more lonely because of her. The sudden thought softened him a little. And it dawned on him how lonely it must have made her to be constantly suspected of cheating on him the whole time they were married. It didn't make it any easier to understand her, but he did feel sorry for having showered her with doubt instead of love. It was possible that, in his drunken state on that last night in his home country, he'd dialed her number and apologized recklessly, or gone to see her in person, or even pleaded for her to come over. As usually happens when one drinks oneself into a stupor, he found himself the next day, on the morning of his flight, burdened with a hangover so massive that he could remember nothing of the night before—along with regret, unexpected muscle pain (he thought maybe he and Yujin had come to blows but could not remember), and dark blue bruises that would take a long time to go away.

The only person he could entrust the dog to was his ex-wife. He was thinking of telling her that she could stay in his apartment if she was having trouble finding new living arrangements after her second divorce. During the six months to five years that he would be spending abroad, he would get several vacations, but he had no intention of returning home for them. His father, who had remarried after his mother died many years ago, was the only family he had, but he felt no particular need to visit him. His apartment was just sitting empty. And since he had to leave it empty for at least half a year, better that she move in while he was gone. Being divorced felt like being one of those weekend couples forced to live in separate cities for work. It filled him with jealousy to have to see Yujin at social gatherings, but when he really thought about it, it wasn't so different from being an older brother who has lost his little sister, with whom he was once very close, to a playboy brother-in-law. In other words, he still thought of his ex-wife as family. The only problem being, he wasn't much of a family man.

He didn't know his ex-wife's phone number. He knew her old number but had not bothered to memorize her new one when she married Yujin. If he could find out Yujin's number, he could track down hers. Of course, he didn't know Yujin's number either, but he knew where he worked, and they would be able to tell him.

He called information in his home country and got the phone number for Yujin's company. A recorded message instructed him to dial the extension for the department he was trying to reach, so he entered the number for human resources. He had no idea what department Yujin worked in. Other than having married and divorced the same woman, he knew little about Yujin. He thought the extension for human resources would connect him directly to an employee, but instead it led to another menu. He didn't know there were so many separate divisions within the human resources department, and of course had no idea whose extension he should enter, so he followed the recorded instructions and pressed a number at random. The phone rang twice before someone answered and recited the name of the division followed by their own name in the friendly voice of a telephone company operator. When he told the employee his name and explained that he was looking for someone's contact information, the employee's voice turned brusque, as if they got that sort of phone call all the time.

"This is not an information center," the voice over the phone said.

He apologized on reflex, but then felt he really did owe the person an apology: clearly they had their hands full at work, and here he was interrupting them for something as trifling as a phone number. And so, in a more gracious voice, he told the person where he was calling from and explained that he had left all of his contact numbers back at home, and that the only way for him to get in touch with his friend was to go through the company directory.

"Wait, you're calling from where? Are you serious?"

Mentioning Country C seemed to have a certain effect.

"Yes, I'm calling long-distance from Country C."

"What's it like?"

He didn't know what to say, so he glanced out the balcony window.

"Um, the weather's nice."

"The weather's nice . . . How 'bout that?"

He was about to say that a contagious disease was going around, that the streets were filled with trash, and that because of the risk of mass infection, he was locked inside of his apartment, but just then the employee asked who he was looking for. He happily recited Yujin's name. It turned out that there were three men with the same name, so he added Yujin's age. Two of the three men were born the same year. Once he added which school Yujin had graduated from, the employee narrowed it down to one. He tightened his grip on his pen, ready to write down the phone number.

"I'm sorry, but I can't give it to you. It's listed under his personal information. I can't just hand out his number or I'll get in trouble," the employee said. His voice had softened.

"I don't think Yujin would get angry at you for telling me his number."

"I'm sure you understand, but the longer you haven't heard from someone, the less welcome their phone calls tend to be. I'll give him your number and ask him to call you instead."

He started to agree that he should do just that, but then he remembered that he did not know his own phone number, and he told the employee he would call back in the afternoon and asked him to try to get Yujin's permission in the mean-time. After hanging up, he thought about what the employee had said, that the longer you haven't heard from someone, the less welcome their phone calls are, and he nodded in agreement.

When he finally called Yujin's cell, having gotten the num-ber from the employee who had gotten permission in turn from Yujin, the phone was turned off. Yujin must have been in a meeting. He waited to be connected to voice mail, where he started to leave a message, speaking calmly as he did so.

"Yujin, sorry to call you like this, but I need to get my ex-wife's number from you."

He paused for a moment, deep in thought, and then continued.

"Never mind. I'll just ask for your help instead. Can you go to my apartment and let my dog out? Just take it outside somewhere and leave it there."

He made sure to add the passcode for his front door at the end of the message, but it was a sudden impulse that had made him ask Yujin to simply let the dog go. He hated having to ask his ex-wife or anyone else to take care of his dog for him, or to find someone who could. Ever since remembering that he had left the dog in the apartment, he had been so overcome with anxiety that he couldn't do anything, couldn't concentrate on any other thoughts, and this made him very unhappy.

It only occurred to him as he was leaving the message that he had absolutely no desire to care for the dog. Nor did he want to start things back up with his ex-wife. He hated the idea of her depending on him, but more than that, he hated the thought of wanting to get back together with her. He knew that the news of his ex-wife and Yujin's divorce had left him giddy with unexpected anticipation. But he refused to be so easily defeated by his own heart.

He doubted Yujin would follow through. Most likely Yujin would snort with laughter and delete the message. But it didn't matter. Given the circumstances he was in, fearing for the dog and worrying about its safety was a luxury. The important thing was to protect himself from the virus raging outside, from the piles of unsanitary garbage filling the streets, from the apartment building crawling with the infected. He had to put everything he had into surviving. In a city where disease spread like bushfire, in a city where pharmacies were put out of business by looters, in a city stalked by mountains of garbage and ghoulish quarantine officers in full-body hazmat suits, in a city where you had to eat whenever a bell went off, he had to keep from getting sick, he had to be ready to work. So no matter how he felt about the dog, and in truth he didn't feel much of anything for it, or how much his ex-wife loved the dog, who really cared if that mutt, lucky enough to be living in a peaceful city, had to go hungry for a few more days?

FIVE

Two days after leaving the message for Yujin, he got a call back. When he thought about it later, those two days were the most peaceful he had spent since his arrival. He thought about the dog often and felt guilty each time he did, was hungry all the time because the meals were too small, grew impatient that Mol had not yet called him, and felt uneasy remembering what Trout had said about there being a problem with his assignment. But looking back on it now, it was time spent indulging in relatively peaceful worries.

When the phone rang, he was overjoyed because he thought it was Mol. He was ready to complain about being confined to his apartment, about how badly he was suffering because he was unable to buy cold medicine, and how he wanted to start work immediately. If Mol knew what he was going through, having to eat rationed meals in that terrible stench, he wouldn't dare refuse him anything.

Even before he put the phone to his ear, he heard his mother tongue. It was Yujin. Not the Mol he was hoping to hear from, but it made him happy nonetheless.

"Yujin!" He pitched his voice exaggeratedly high as he remembered how impulsively he'd asked Yujin to take care of his dog despite how strained things were between them and the fact that they'd never been close to begin with. "Thanks, man. You saved me."

"I saved you? Then I guess you killed me."

"What are you talking about? And hey, how did you get this number? What *is* the number anyway?"

"You called me, remember? The number showed up on my cell phone. I couldn't tell where it was from. You have no idea how long I've been trying to call. It took me forever to remember that you were in Country C. I guess that proves we're not friends. But you knew that, right?"

"I know, and thank you, seriously. I'm grateful to you for wasting all that time on my behalf. You really did me a favor, so thank you." He got embarrassed at how he kept gushing at Yujin, who still had no idea of the situation he was in, and asked in a more even voice, "How did it go with the dog?"

"I was going to just abandon it somewhere, like you told me to do. I had zero intention of taking care of your dog. I don't know what you thought, but we're not close enough for you to be asking me for a favor like that. Frankly, I was pissed off that you would leave such a rude message."

"I know," he said weakly. He had not wanted to put Yujin in a bad mood.

"And yet you left that message, like you were giving me an order . . ."

"I was so sure you would ignore it."

"I went to your house because, if I couldn't kick your ass, then I could at least kick your dog. Calm myself down that way."

"I hope you kicked it and kept kicking it until you felt better."

"I didn't have to."

"Why? Did it bite you?"

He pictured Yujin getting bit by the dog and grinned to himself.

"I bet you wished it bit me, but that wasn't it."

"Then it ran away? I shut the door pretty tight."

"No, it didn't run away."

"Then what?"

"You seriously don't know? I've given you more than enough time to explain yourself."

"I have no idea what you're talking about."

"I thought you knew. I didn't understand why you'd left me that message until I got to your house and saw for myself."

"Look, Yujin. I had no intention of asking you to take care of the dog. I was only planning to ask for my ex-wife's phone number. I don't have anyone's contact information with me right now, so I had to call you in order to get her number. But then—"

"Enough excuses. I saw what you wanted me to see."

"All I asked you to do was take one whiny mutt out of an empty house and get rid of it. It wasn't as big a favor to ask as you're making it sound. It's not like I asked you for a kidney or some—"

"It was dead."

"What?"

"It was dead."

"Dead? The dog?"

"Yeah."

"Are you sure it wasn't just sleeping?"

"I'm sure."

"Did you mistake it for me and throw it out the window?"

"That is the worst joke I have ever heard," Yujin said, his voice sounding strangely flat.

"You know, it probably ate everything in sight after I left. That dog never could stand to go hungry. It must have made itself sick."

"Maybe so, but that's not how it died."

"The dog's really dead?"

"It was stabbed. Cut to shreds."

Yujin's voice shook. It was the voice of someone seized with fear. If Yujin had said that while sounding cold and distant, like everything else he had said up until that point, the man would have burst out laughing. He might have even mimicked Yujin and told him it was the cruelest joke he had ever heard. But Yujin wasn't the joking type. He was more inclined to mistake his friends' jokes to mean they were making fun of him and get angry instead.

"There was something else, besides the dog."

"What?"

"Are you *seriously* telling me you don't know?"

"The only things in my house that had lives to lose were the dog and the cockroaches. Oh, and ants. In the winter, I get these long lines of little red ants, they look just like threads, right near the boiler."

"Better get a good grip on the phone then, you might drop it in shock."

Yujin pretended to be warning him, but he paused dramatically, as if hoping the man really would be shocked. Or maybe Yujin was catching his breath and trying to calm his own fear. After giving the man plenty of time to feel scared while trying to figure out what else was dead in his apartment besides the dog, the cockroaches, and the ants, Yujin slowly sounded out the words:

"Our ex-wife."

The man couldn't help but laugh. It was a rotten joke, to bring his ex-wife into it.

"Now that's the worst joke *I've* ever heard, Yujin. I don't know if you realize, but I am in no shape right now to listen to dumb jokes. If you keep messing around like this, you're just asking to get chewed out."

"I'm telling the truth."

"I—"

"She was stabbed. A lot. Her face was mashed up, like she'd been stabbed in the face over and over. If it weren't for the clothes she was wearing, I would have had no idea who she was. It was that bad . . ."

He thought Yujin was done, but after a moment, he heard muffled sobs. The sound was faint, frail. Like the weeping of some injured animal. Yujin was crying. The man felt like his stomach and other organs had fallen right out of his body. Yujin was not joking. Nobody could joke that way and then cry like that.

"She's dead?"

Yujin continued to cry quietly as he tried to speak.

"I was sure you knew."

Why would Yujin think that? He didn't say anything for a moment, and then he suddenly understood, and this time he felt like his arms and legs had fallen off. He had never, not even once, wished his ex-wife were dead, so of course he had never so much as dreamed of killing her. Yes, there were many times when he had hated her or wished she would vanish right before his eyes, but that was only a desire for physical distance, not her biological extinction.

"I had to go to the police station again today."

"Did you say the police?" Now he was the one with the shaking voice.

"I couldn't not report what I saw! I was scared."

"I'm more afraid of what you're thinking right now." He spoke quietly just in case the trembling in his voice would sound like proof that Yujin's suspicions of him were correct. But it only made it worse. He sounded like he was crying.

"I played your voice message for the police. So they would understand what I was doing in your apartment in the first place. They're investigating different leads now for why our ex-wife would be found dead in your apartment."

"I have absolutely no idea how she got there."

"I thought you'd be able to tell me something." In an instant, the tears vanished from Yujin's voice, and it turned as dry and stiff as a bolt of cotton. "But you aren't saying anything. You just keep repeating what I say."

"There's nothing for me to say. I have no idea what happened."

"Whether you know what happened or not, I couldn't just leave her body there. If I did, there would have been trouble later for sure. Because I'm the one who reported it, they kept me in for questioning and they're going to continue investigating me."

The man thought about the space between the words "couldn't just leave her body there" and "trouble later for sure."

"Who in the world would do such a thing?"

"I can't answer that. But I do have one thing to say to you: I hope that you'll try to do what is legal, and moral."

"Everything I do is legal and moral," the man said and sighed. He didn't enjoy being lectured by Yujin when they weren't even close, and in the kind of voice you would expect only the strictest of parents to use.

Yujin sighed as well and said, "If that's true, then good luck convincing the police."

Yujin slammed down the receiver before the man could respond. After a moment, he heard the dial tone that signaled the phone call had ended.

She's dead. She's dead. She's dead. She's dead. She's dead. She's dead. She's dead.

He mumbled the words over and over, but the more he repeated them, the less real it felt. Yujin's phone call was just a mean joke. Clearly, Yujin suspected that the man had slept with his ex-wife while she was married to Yujin, and had spent the last few days trying to think of how best to hurt him.

He opened the balcony door. As the smell of trash and fumigant slowly spread into the room, a stunned sorrow spread out from the center of his body. It was not the sorrow of realizing that she was dead. It was something similar to what he had felt as a child, when he stood before the dark funeral portrait of his deceased mother. He had not seen his mother's body. No one in his family wanted him, just a boy at the time, to see what she looked like when she died, her body mangled from the traffic accident. Though he was still a child, he knew what death was, but he did not yet understand what it meant to lose a mother.

He'd felt sad because of his father. Dressed in a black suit that was too heavy for the season, his father dripped with sweat in the funeral home. The boy couldn't stop glancing at his father in that suit. It had been made for his parents' wedding nine years earlier. A furniture wholesaler, his father normally wore jeans and a windbreaker. Other than attending other people's weddings, he never had any reason to wear a suit. The jacket sleeves were too tight on his father, who had gained a potbelly after marriage, and the pants were wrinkled from kneeling to bow each time people stood before his mother's funeral portrait to pay their condolences, and from sitting back like a stone with his back slumped when they left. The sleeves tightened like sausages each time he leaned forward and looked like they were going to burst; by the afternoon of the second day, the seam in the armpit gave way and the white shirt underneath bulged out like a white-coated tongue. Everyone was too sad to care or to laugh. The sorrow of mourning the dead helped them to overlook the absurd. The boy kept glancing at the white fabric. It looked like his mother sticking her tongue out at him to keep him from crying.

Later that night, after the boy had fallen asleep in the reception hall where several guests were still quietly tilting back glasses of alcohol, he was awakened by the sound of stifled sobs. His father sat alone in front of his mother's portrait, crying. The boy burst into tears at the sight. He cried because of the quiet funeral hall, because of the peppery smell of the beef soup that had thickened and condensed from boiling too long, because of the dark faces of the tired people, because of his father crying until his eyes turned red. He cried, not out of mourning for a deceased mother, but from the sorrow of witnessing his father's humble face now contorted and clownish, his bald head beaded with sweat, his one good suit torn.

About a month after the funeral, his father called a cleaning lady to help straighten up their neglected house. As she was cleaning the refrigerator, she made a face and took out the containers of side dishes one by one and set them on the table. They were the last dishes the boy's mother had made. They had turned moldy and sour with rot. The boy jumped out from where he'd been hiding in his room, watching as she cleaned, and grabbed one of the containers before she could dump it out. It was stir-fried dried shrimp, his least favorite of the side dishes. He couldn't stand the way the shells always got stuck between his teeth when he ate it. He stood there, glowering at the hateful cleaning lady and stuffing his mouth full of moldy shrimp.

For several days, he had a raging stomachache. With no one to take care of him, he had to suffer through it alone, the diarrhea wearing away at his bottom, while he realized at last that his mother was gone. Pain spread through his body and his heart, rising up and down his esophagus with each nauseating whiff of the moldy, mushy shrimp. He lay sick in bed alone late into the night and accepted the fact that he would have to nurse himself back from illness without his mother.

His ex-wife's death would sink in the same way. Only after his entire body ached because of her, only after all of the words that he wanted to say and needed to say had backed up inside of him and turned his stomach while his tongue stiffened with pain from not being able to speak even a single word since she was not there to hear them, would it finally become real. So he was not sad because his ex-wife had died. What he felt was nothing more than the dismay of being informed unilaterally by someone who was more stranger than friend, in a voice laced with suspicion, and while he was stranded in a foreign country, that the person he was closest to in this world had died.

He longed to talk to his ex-wife, more than he ever had before. He had to keep repeating the words "she's dead" to himself, if only to shake off that thought. Even if he couldn't get it through his head, she was obviously not there with him so he couldn't have talked to her anyway.

He had strayed once, before the divorce. The girl was friendly and laughed easily, and she liked him. For a while, he was secretly tormented, wondering whether he loved the girl, while also trying to figure out whether the girl loved him back. He would think he was madly in love one day, but then the next day think to himself that if this flimsy emotion was called love, then he may as well say he loved a dog on the street. Unable to make up his mind, he slept with the girl several more times.

What bothered him was not guilt or the moral failing of sleeping with someone else while legally married. Nor did he feel any remorse toward his wife, or the girl he kept sleeping with despite not knowing whether he loved her or not. What weighed on him was the loneliness of not being able to talk about the affair with his wife. It was the loneliness of one who harbors a secret he would prefer not to carry. When it came to the waves of feeling that washed over him, the thrill he felt each time he saw the girl, the insecurity of not knowing if she was going to leave him, the anxiety of wanting to be loved by her, the loneliness of having to guess what she was feeling through a single trivial word as she never opened up to him completely, and the fact that he wanted to get away from her despite all of that, the only person he wanted to confide in was his wife. After listening to the whole story, his wife, more than anyone else, would have been able to tell him whether or not the girl loved him, whether or not he loved the girl, and just how hard that love would make things for him in the end. But he also knew it was precisely for that reason that the one person he could never tell was his wife.

He felt as lonely now as he had then. He longed to talk to his ex-wife about her death and about how hurt he was that she had fled to a world so disconnected from his own. But the one who would have been even more eager to talk about her death was his ex-wife herself. She would have wanted to tell him how terrified she was the moment she sensed her end was coming, how exquisite the pain was when the knife entered her flesh (he started to cry for the first time as he pictured it), how horrifying to realize she was still alive after being stabbed repeatedly, and how frightening to release her final breath as she used the last of her strength to open her eyes and gaze up at her killer. As lonely as he felt at being unable to tell her about his loneliness, she must have felt just as lonely at being unable to tell anyone about her death.

His tears fell, but her death still felt unreal to him. It would have been no different if her corpse were spread out right before his eyes. But because he was no longer a boy, he accepted her death as a fact separate from feeling, and ached as he pictured her suffering. He could never see his ex-wife again, could never share a conversation with her again. The chance to talk to her about the loneliness of keeping secrets from each other, the profound loneliness that came from only sharing what seemed appropriate, that chance was lost to him forever.

The man took out his laptop. He had been using it sparingly. The battery had just over an hour left on it. The charger was, of course, in his stolen suitcase. In an hour, the laptop would be useless. Internet access was so unstable that it took a long time to get online, and even then, the connection was bad and kept cutting out. He struggled to find out what was happening in Country C. Other than reports that the virus was spreading quickly, there was little news. The problem of neglected garbage, looting, and quarantining appeared to be confined to District 4. There were sixteen major cities in Country C, including City Y, which was further divided into twenty-four different districts. No wonder the national news made no mention of District 4, when it was such a tiny part of Country C.

Meanwhile, news of his ex-wife's murder was splashed all over the headlines back home. It pained him to see her name followed by her age (far too young an age to die), statements that she had been found with multiple stab wounds, which suggested that she'd been murdered out of spite, and speculation over what she might have done at such a young age to have such enemies. He felt his heart was going to burst. And just as Yujin had said, the man was pegged as the prime suspect. The fact that her body was found in his apartment, the fact that right after the incident (it was estimated that the crime had been committed the day he left) he had fled to another country (though it was absurd to call what he did fleeing), and the fact that the knife found in the compost bin outside his apartment building was the same kind he used at home and had traces of blood that appeared to be his ex-wife's along the blade were all evidence that pointed to him. Not a single fingerprint had been found on the knife handle, so it was presumed that he had tried to carefully remove any evidence before disposing of it.

No one in their right mind would toss a murder weapon so close to home, and yet the police had fingered him anyway. They liked to wrap up investigations as quickly as possible and would brand their first suspect as guilty. They would be so thirsty for his blood that they wouldn't even consider other possibilities. Some officers would stop at nothing to lock up a suspect.

He looked down expectantly at his bruised palm and forearms, the soreness now all but faded, as if they might tell him something. It was possible the bruises meant he'd had something to do with his ex-wife's death, just as the police conjectured. But then it occurred to him that he'd forgotten to leave his address in his voice mail to Yujin, and yet Yujin had gone straight there. The only person who knew that address was his ex-wife, and she was already dead by then. Yujin had never been to his apartment before, had not asked how to get there, and had not been told. The man wondered how he had found it at all.

What if that night, after the man blacked out, Yujin, who was relatively sober, had helped him home? What if in his drunken state he had called his ex-wife and demanded that she come over? And though it wouldn't have been what he had in mind to do, what if he had laid into her when she showed up, and blamed her for all of their failures? What if all three of them had started bickering because of that? And what if, at the end of all that bickering, secrets were revealed and, unable to bear the pain caused by those secrets, one of them had grabbed a knife?

There was the problem, too, of the knife, which was said to have been stained with her blood and supposedly found in the compost bin of his apartment building. He hated taking out the compost. The bins were always disgusting, the air stank for several feet around them, and cats were always jumping out at him when he least expected it. After the divorce, he'd gone to great lengths to avoid generating any food waste. When it could not be helped, he would wrap his leftover food in a plastic bag and throw it away surreptitiously in the trash can in front of the convenience store on his way to work instead. In fact, he wasn't even entirely sure where the compost bin was. So, if the knife had been thrown away, it must have been Yujin who did it. Besides, on the morning of his departure, he was rushing from room to room, packing his bags, and yet he had not seen his wife's body. He'd been in too much of a hurry to go through the entire apartment, but there was no way he could have missed the smell of blood or any other signs of foul play. If his ex-wife died in his apartment, then it had to have happened after he left the country.

He kept thinking that someone like Yujin was definitely capable of killing his ex-wife, but that, on the other hand, not even Yujin was capable of that. Yujin was impatient, was prone to flying off the handle and verbally lashing out, had a habit of clenching his fists to work off his anger, and had aimed those fists at others on more than one occasion. The man had personally witnessed Yujin's fists flying through the air at other people, and had found himself on the receiving end. If Yujin had found out that he and his ex-wife were still sleeping together after their divorce, he would not have taken it well. It may have been a cliché to be cuckolded by your wife and your best friend, but it wasn't so funny once it happened to you. That said, killing someone was completely different from swinging a fist, breaking a window, tossing a chair, or lashing out with words. Even someone who couldn't control his anger and assaulted people out of habit was not necessarily a killer. Yujin may have been quick to explode with rage, but he was not so cruel as to stab a person over and over.

Having finished his clumsy detective work, the man shook his head. Regardless of whether he or Yujin was the culprit, there was no way he could have blacked it out so completely, no matter how much he'd drunk that night. This wasn't some childhood nightmare that you forgot once you were all grown up. You didn't forget a thing like that.

He grabbed some of his rationed bread and chewed it slowly. It was sweet. His sense of taste bothered him. How could bread still taste sweet at a time like this? But he tore off pieces of the hard bread with his teeth anyway, took his time chewing, and swallowed it slowly, bite by bite. That was all he could do for now to keep himself alive.

He recalled that while he was drunk he had been clutching something in his hand the same way he was now clutching the bag of bread. That had to be where the bruise on his palm had come from. The last piece of bread that he had so optimistically put in his mouth got stuck in his throat, and he finally had to spit it out. What was in his hand that night? He couldn't be sure. This was not a problem of memory but of sensation.

He walked around the house, picking up things that he might have held that night: a heavy ballpoint pen, a rolled-up notebook, a hard leather pencil case, wooden chopsticks. All sorts of items, one after the other. Then, though he did not want to, he took the kitchen knife out of the sink and squeezed the handle. When he gripped the curved handle of the knife, his palm trembled, as if recognizing a feeling that was at once strange and familiar. Fearful of that tremor, he released his grip. The knife fell to the floor.

The dropped knife was as stiff as the look on his face. He opened and closed his empty hand. Just because the knife had felt familiar, just because he could still feel it in his hand, just because his hand remembered the exact sensation of it, did not mean that he had stabbed his ex-wife. Knife handles were all the same, any one of them would feel familiar at first. But regardless of the truth, the moment he picked up the knife and let it fall, the moment that uncanny tremor ran through his body, he felt the world coming toward him, a world as cold as a blade and as blunt as the heel of a knife.

The doorbell rang. He wasn't expecting anyone, and in fact he'd never even heard the doorbell before, so it took several rings before he realized the sound was coming from his own apartment. Slowly and carefully, so as not to make a sound, he tiptoed over and looked through the peephole. Three men were standing in a semicircle, blocking the door. All three were dressed in street clothes and wore dust masks.

He assumed they were from the disaster management headquarters, visiting him as part of the quarantine procedures. The police had said the apartment building was on lockdown so that they could determine which of the residents were infected and take them to a separate center for treatment. On the afternoon of the first day of quarantine, he'd had blood drawn so they could test him for infection. They had told him the results would take a while, but maybe they were ready early. Or maybe the men were here because of his quarantine in the airport. The public health inspector there had told him not to leave his place of sojourn as they might visit him for a follow-up diagnosis. But they could also be detectives who had come to arrest the prime suspect in a murder case. They would have figured out right away where he was, and Country C had an extradition treaty with his home country.

"Who's there?"

He checked to make sure the door was locked before slowly walking over to the balcony and calling out in his native language. One of the men standing outside said his name. His name was difficult for foreigners to pronounce, especially for people from Country C, but the person outside not only understood him but also enunciated his name clearly. It had to be someone from the same country as him. They could have been from the company, but no one at the head office spoke his mother tongue fluently, and if they had to contact him, they would have used the phone. If this was to inform him of the results of his blood test or because something had been added to the quarantine procedure, then it would be a local health inspector, someone dressed in a hazmat suit, someone unable to pronounce his name correctly.

The three men pounded on the door and called out his name with perfect pronunciation. If he went with them back to his home country, with these men he was assuming were detectives, he would lose any chance to prove his innocence. He was a suspect, but he was not guilty. He could still feel the knife in his hand, but he knew he had not used it. And yet that was secondary. The main problem before him was the fact that he was their prime suspect. It was childish, wishful thinking for him to hope they would know he was innocent simply because he was.

He opened the balcony door and looked down. A sprayer truck must have just passed by: clouds of disinfectant roiled up from below. Crows flew past in the dark and lowering sky. He couldn't see the ground through all that vapor, but he knew it would be piled high with black garbage bags giving off their vile yet familiar stench. They would break his fall. It was better than not knowing whether anything was down there at all, better than jumping with blind hope. The moment was so brief. He had no time to think or decide, pushed only by the instinctive fear that said he must not get caught. But he believed there was more to what he did next than simply his not being a criminal. Though he did not know it yet, he would have to suffer for a very long time the disillusionment of knowing that, in the end, he alone had reduced himself to garbage. He heard a keycard slide into the lock. They must have gotten it from the building super-intendent. The deadbolt would slow them for a moment, but soon that too would slide open. Just as the door swung wide, he stifled another cough and leapt into the garbage below.

PART TWO

ONE

In his home country, the man was a product developer at a pest control firm. Despite the job title, he didn't actually research and develop products himself. All he really did was take the pesticides created at their company headquarters abroad, run safety checks to ensure they met local quality standards, and prepare new product launches. Their products were highly toxic. The basic principle behind the company's rodenticide had not changed since its first iteration fifty years ago, but the toxicity had grown and grown. And yet rats refused to go extinct.

The human endeavor known as rat-catching may as well be called a history of failure. The more powerful the toxins, the thicker the coveralls and the more fearsome the gas masks were that you had to wear each time you used them. Experts offered up one idea after another for catching rats, but all they gained was the realization that the harder they tried to eradicate them, the more likely they were to end up hurting people instead. Of course, the bright ideas those experts came up with were to spray rats with the rabies virus or intentionally spread the bubonic plague, effectively killing rats, yes, but taking down far more people in the process.

The commonly used term for the one who administered the pesticide was "exterminator" and the industry itself was referred to as "extermination," but those names presented problems. They raised customers' expectations too high, gave false hope that pests could be eliminated completely. Rats, in particular, cannot be exterminated. If it can be wiped out with mere poison or traps, then it's not a rat to begin with.

Once you know how rats spend their time, the reason for this becomes clear. Rats devote their lives to propagating the species. It is their sole act of production. They can mate dozens of times a day, and a female rat can birth a new litter every month, churning out over a hundred pups a year. They can turn any place into their own territory, and it takes only a single female for them to colonize.

After "extermination" fell out of favor, most companies went through several name changes before landing on the current "pest control" and "environmental hygiene." Specialized terms like "rat catcher" were useless because environmental hygiene and pest control does not select for a single species but rather targets all pests at the same time. And they had to consider the clients' point of view. "Environmental hygiene" had a satisfying ring to it that assured customers they were leaving the matter in the hands of experts, whereas "rat catcher" was unpleasant and conjured up images of unsanitary working conditions. Say the word "hygiene" and you picture a freshly scrubbed kitchen sink; say the words "rat catcher" and you picture a dirty bathroom drain, a sewer.

Nevertheless, aside from routine pest control for homes and apartments, the man's company's biggest problem was still rats. One look at the company logo was enough to tell: a red circle with a slash through it enclosed a dark, evil-looking rat with its teeth bared. The logo practically screamed annihilation of rat-kind.

In the early days, those who specialized in killing rats had only clumsy tools at their disposal—clubs and sticks, or large traps that slammed shut at the slightest touch. They crawled into places no one else cared to enter: dank basements, dust-filled attics, filthy storage sheds where towering piles of odds and ends threatened to topple over and bury them. Today's rat catchers no longer have to stalk alleyways after dark, barehanded or swinging long clubs, while they wait for a rat to randomly scurry out. Certainly no need to practice playing the pipe. Luring rats into a river to drown by twiddling on a magic pipe only happens in storybooks.

You might question whether cities are truly so overrun with rats that they require an entire profession dedicated to the task, but no matter where you are, there are always more rats than you think. It's a mistake to assume that because you've never seen a rat at home, there are none. Rats can be found in places where they have been spotted, where they've never been spotted, and even where you think they couldn't possibly ever be spotted. They are anywhere and everywhere.

We think of a city as an aboveground space made up externally of buildings and homes and bridges and all manner of shops, but it is also a hidden, underground space of sewer tunnels and conduits for buried power lines. These conduits are the rats' alleyways. If aboveground is the world of people, then below is the world of rats. The deep structure of the city resembles a distribution chart of its teeming rodent population.

But while every city is full of rats, you won't spot them just anywhere. In all but the most unusual of cases, rats will not walk down the sidewalk in broad daylight. They will not because they have not. Rats take only familiar roads, most of which are secluded paths, dark alleys. Everything looks different from the other side.

Sprawling parks and luxurious flowerbeds. Tiny parks and cramped flowerpots. Dirt yards of abandoned houses. Well-kept gardens and lawns. Basements stuffed with belongings. Under floorboards. In the sewer. Under old furniture. Inside rolled up carpets. Anywhere that looks like a hole or a pit is where the rat makes its home. Even in the subway stations used by thousands of people every day, rats coolly seek out the dark places beneath the tracks and in the tunnels to line their nests.

If you have ever spotted a rat where you live, then know that forty-eight more were hiding just out of sight. Or fifty-six. Or sixty-seven. In fact, whatever your least favorite two or three-digit number is (the higher the number, the likelier the odds) that's the number you should think of. But the exact count doesn't really matter. You will never catch every hidden rat. What matters is knowing there are far more rats than the ones you actually see. So, if you think catching the one rat that you can see is difficult, don't even dream of catching the countless hidden others. It is not a problem of numbers. It is a problem of power. The rat that you see is always the weakest of its colony. It is too weak to find food on its own turf—that is, in your basements and subway tunnels, in your sewers and buried conduits—and are forced to venture out into the unknown in search of food. If you can't catch them, then what makes you think you could catch the others?

The truth is, rats die all the time without the help of exterminators. City rats die for as many different reasons as people die. They get run over in the street, or sucked up drainpipes by toilet plungers and drown. Some are snatched up by birds, and some, despite living in a trash-strewn city, fail at finding food and simply starve.

Rats sometimes die in traps, but their pathological dislike of the unknown makes this method difficult. Rats are intensely conservative and suspicious of anything new or unfamiliar. Poison is far more common. Poison shuts down the rat's body and makes it unable to digest food. Blood circulation to the lungs slows, and the rats drag themselves out of the dark and into the bright outdoors in search of air. Poison also has the advantage of killing a large number at one time. And yet, while countless rats can be slain in this fashion, the effect is transitory. No matter what poison you use, there will always be rats that develop a resistance. There are even rats that can survive the destruction of an entire colony. There always are. For the minority that survives, their fertility rate skyrockets. And less competition for food means they get bigger, stronger. So the harder you try to eradicate them, the better an environment you create for the survivors. Threats of extinction only strengthen the species.

It is the same for humans. No virus can kill the entire population. Even if 99.99 percent of people were to die, the survivors who have natural immunity would live. Epidemics are like rat poison: they strengthen the race by leaving behind only the strongest rats. And just like rats, the human species is not easily exterminated.

The garbage dump is at its most beautiful when the garbage is on fire. Particularly in the early mornings, when a thin fog or faint clouds of fumigant still hang in the air, the glow rising from the trash is as beautiful as a sunset on a clear day. The fire blooms a dusky rose, the color complementing the clean morning air. It starts off a bit hazy, but the color gradually clarifies until it bursts into full flame, black smoke belching forth. The smoke that rises when everything in the world burns. Going up in smoke along with the household garbage discarded by the city's inhabitants are the rats that get picked up with the garbage and cannot escape the pyre, as well as corpses that can no longer be accommodated at the hospital and are secretly discarded in the middle of the night (or so rumors would have it) and the infected who are not yet dead but are already as good as dead (as those rumors would have it). As the fire dies down, the last anemic embers flare when a breeze passes over them and then burn down to nothing, and petals of dark ash are carried on the wind.

After the smoke clears, milky clouds of fumigant mix with the ash and blanket the park. Because of the regular, unceasing intervals of fumigation, the world is always this milky white, as if a veil has been drawn over everything. The constant spraying is the city's sole response to the epidemic. By the time the spray settles, it is the middle of the night or very early, just before dawn, and the park is too dark to make out anything anyway.

The vagrants' day begins with garbage trucks lumbering through the chemical fog to dump their towering loads of refuse. According to the placard posted at the park entrance, this used to be where children played basketball or pick-up games of lacrosse, but as the illness spread and trash disposal became more urgent, it was turned into a temporary site for burning garbage.

Rummaging through discarded things that spilled from the dump still glowing with embers and dark with ash made the man feel like he had become a rat. By the time he managed to pick out something useful, he would be gray with ash from head to toe, the same gray as a rat's fur. And just like rats, he and the other park vagrants owed their survival to the trash.

As the man picked through the rubbish, he was reminded again and again that he was not competing with the other homeless men for survival, he was competing with the rats. He was no match for them. The rats were always faster. They moved freely in the places his arms could not reach and were always first to the places he could reach. They found things he could not find, ate things he could not eat, and got to the things he could eat faster than him.

There was no question that he was lower than a rat now. Like rats, he slept in the open air and foraged through filthy and unspeakable things in search of food, but he was inferior to rats in that they could eat anything whereas he ate whatever he found only to suffer repeated illness.

Though he could not compete with the rats and the other homeless, he liked the dump. It had everything he needed: a change of clothes, shoes, a broken umbrella, paper or fabric bags to hold his personal effects (that is, the cracked bowl and comb he'd collected after his first few days of being homeless), and even a suitcase. The most important thing though was food. The dump provided him with

CITY OF ASH AND RED

long-expired bread turned moldy, overcooked noodles that had dried flat, wilted vegetables that had lost their color. Sometimes he got lucky and found perfectly good food that had been tossed out. The smell made it easy to find. Whenever he caught the foul stench of rot coming from somewhere in the trash, odds were good that he would find something there that had once been called food. The smell of spoil and rot was the smell of sustenance.

For the first few days following his arrival in the park, the man had eaten almost nothing. He had been too busy feeling sorry for himself and wondering why he should be reduced to foraging for rotten crumbs. But he soon realized that feeling sorry for himself did nothing to curb his hunger. As a vagrant, he could not afford this inhibition toward food. The first time hunger drove him to forage through a garbage can, the terrible smell did not bother him because he was too busy holding back his tears. He ate rotten, sludgy noodles. Once he got the first bite down, the rest was easy. If there were bugs, he picked them off and ate. If it was spoiled, he plugged his nose and ate.

When he discovered a knife etched with the logo of an airline company in a pile of ashes one day, he felt that he had finally gotten one over on the rats. Not that a rat would have any use for a knife. Fearful someone might take it from him, he checked his surroundings and slipped it into his pocket. The blade was dull and hardly distinguishable from the spine. All it was really good for was spreading butter on toast. But whenever he lay faceup on his park bench in the middle of the night and could not tell whether the haze that blurred his vision was caused by the constant fumigation or the sleep gumming up his eyes, or because he was crying, and whenever another homeless man snatched up a bit of trash that he had had his eye on, and whenever he went after that other homeless man only to be beaten and knocked back, he would slip his hand down into his pocket and stroke the knife. The cold vitality of the knife's edge gave him courage.

He wondered if he might luck into finding his lost suitcase, but that had not yet happened. Now and then he did come across black suitcases like his. They were useful for storing the things needed in the life of a vagrant, so fights were always breaking out over who would claim them. Time and again, he took a beating and had to weakly bow out, satisfying himself with merely checking whether it was his suitcase or not. He didn't necessarily want his suitcase back. Even if it were his, there was no chance it still contained the items he had brought from his home country. It was hopeless. His suitcase was only so much garbage now. Just as it had taken only a few days for him to become no different from the city's homeless.

Each time the sharp smell of urine pricked his nose, he looked around in fear. The smell came from the garbage fire, from the bench he sat on, from the trees at the center of the park, from the beggars at his side, from the air he breathed, from the ground he walked on. The smell came from all of those things and from him. His bold leap into the garbage bags to escape the men he assumed were detectives had been a fitting prophecy of his future spent digging through garbage. He had sprained his lower back in the fall but had no time to attend to it as he dove into the only hiding space available: between and under the bags of garbage. Then he'd crawled along the ground of this new world, which was populated by bugs and maggots and flowing with a sticky discharge. He kept expecting the detectives to grab him by the scruff of the neck at any moment. The police surrounding the building would surely help the detectives in their search and drag him out of the trash. His heart had raced with fear, and its audible pounding made it difficult for him to make out any other sounds around him. If caught, he would be deported, arrested, tried, branded a criminal, and punished. To avoid being caught, he had shoved his way through garbage and curled up and hid like garbage among the garbage.

If it had not been for the sprayer truck passing by, if the truck had not been spewing out a tremendous cloud of fumigant right at that moment, if the billowing cloud had not perfectly concealed him, he no doubt would have been caught. He snuck onto the roof of the truck as it slowed down to spray the garbage nearby. A second large cloud billowed out, and the truck slowly moved to its next spot, carrying him on its roof. He lifted his head to look back, but all he saw were black garbage bags wreathed in white vapor.

He had planned to stay on top of the truck until he put a good distance between himself and the detectives. If he could, he would have liked to stay on that roof for the rest of his life, his body hidden in the clouds, but he couldn't hold on. His arms and legs hurt too much, and so he'd jumped down and ducked into the park. His muscles were stiff from the effort to press flat against the curved top of the tank-like truck and cling to it with all four limbs. It vexed him to know that he'd been unable to bear a little pain, even in a life-or-death situation. It wasn't as if he had been dying of pain either, it was more of a constant, nagging discomfort. He lay down on the first empty bench he saw and thought, if he were to die, it would not be from a virus or a knife to the heart. More likely he would grow careless and tread on a rusty nail and die of tetanus. A part of him preferred the idea. He deserved to die slowly and by something so stupid and trivial.

When he wasn't picking through garbage, he passed the time like the other homeless men: lying or sitting or slumped on his bench. He did not feel real. If he didn't keep his back pressed to the bench, he became a puff of air. His cold lingered. Whenever he grew tired, the coughing fits returned, squeezing his chest. His head ached all the time from the fumigant, and he had an unbearable itch somewhere. His skin turned ashy and flaky, and scabs formed over the spots that he could not resist scratching. When he ran his nails over the scabs, they bled. The undersides of his overgrown fingernails turned black from the dead skin and dandruff that collected there each time he scratched his head.

Seventeen vagrants lived in the park, one for each bench. The bench under the streetlight nearest the entrance was number one, and the rest followed clockwise. He had no idea who had numbered the benches, but he found this out when he overheard one of the others refer to him as Nine and the man across from him as Eleven.

They had numbers, but they rarely addressed each other. He knew his number and that was all; no one called out and no one responded. Other than Three and Six, who were always mumbling something under their breath, the sound a constant singsong hum, the rest of the homeless men were remarkable for their utter silence. Was the refusal to move from their seats due to the fear of becoming infected, or simply the vagrants' way of claiming ownership? Either way, they only spoke to each other when they fought over a piece of garbage, and they spent as much time as possible rooted in one spot. And though such cause never arose, even if there had been reason to, they would not have helped each other or saved each other's places or willingly relinquished a single scrap of food pulled from the trash.

On second thought, the constant mumbling might not have come from Three and Six. It could have been Four and Twelve, or even One and Seventeen, who were a bit farther away. The thick fog that hung over the park made it difficult to track exactly where sounds were coming from. Each time the sprayer trucks passed by, the fog grew so dense that he could not see the bench right next to his.

It was difficult, even without the fog, to tell the homeless men apart. All of them were filthy and dressed in rags, their faces hidden behind scruffy beards. Their hair was tangled, their skin blackened with dirt. Their dirtiness was not proportionate to how long they had been homeless. In fact, the shorter their vagrancy, the dirtier they were, whereas the longer they had been out there, the more skilled they were at finding a change of clothes and shoes in the trash, and the more places they knew they could go to wash up, including public bathrooms that were open all night, vacant homes for rent that were left unlocked, and apartment construction sites that they could enter after dark, which meant they could keep themselves relatively clean if they wanted to.

Their numbers were not permanent. The numbers belonged not to their persons but to the benches. After the person who had sat on the second bench lost his spot, he kicked someone else off of the sixth bench and became Six.

This losing and taking of benches was an everyday occurrence. Arguments over seats led to indiscriminate blows, but no one ever tried to intervene. Once a new vagrant had occupied a seat, a string of fights would follow: the loser would simply move to another bench and pick a fight with whoever looked weaker than him, and then that loser would do the

CITY OF ASH AND RED

same. All seventeen benches were always occupied, and it was difficult to tell the seventeen faces apart amid the clouds of fumigant and smoke from the garbage fire. There was no way to tell who was sitting where after each fight, and no one ever bothered to ask.

As the fights grew more vicious, they resorted to randomly grabbing bags dumped by the garbage trucks, taking them back to their benches, and rummaging through them there. This reduced their odds of finding anything worthwhile, but it made it easier to protect their seats. Of course, this came to nothing if someone simply decided to attack them and take the seat by force. As the items they dug up proved more and more worthless, the trash strewn throughout the park steadily accumulated. It was soon barely distinguishable from the makeshift landfill nearby.

The man's hardest moments were when it rained at night. It was impossible to stay warm once he was drenched with rain. His only recourse was to squeeze into the space underneath the bench. Lying there on the wet ground, he remembered how happy he had been during his short time quarantined in the apartment. The hot water was shut off, but still he could bathe whenever he wanted, and though the tap water came out rusty, he could filter it and not have to go thirsty. Eating at the sound of a bell like some kind of trained animal was humiliating, but the food always arrived at the same time

125

and tasted the same way, so he never had to worry about going hungry. He could stretch out on his bed and sleep, and if he closed the balcony door, he could block out most of the smell. He was not rained on, never worried about heavy wind, and did not have to slip a hand into his pocket to make sure it still held a knife.

Of course, there had been far happier times in his life than when he was on lockdown. So many, in fact, that he'd had no idea how happy he was then. Now that he lay curled beneath a bench like an insect, the dampness of the earth radiating up at him and cold drops of rain seeping through the wooden slats above, he thought that every single moment in his life but this one had been happy. Even his most torturous moments—like the moment he saw the news and knew with objective certainty that his ex-wife was dead, and those other moments, just on the edge of waking, when he was not sure whether his nightly dream of murdering his ex-wife was only a dream or a lost memory—even those seemed happy in comparison.

He dreamed that she whispered a secret to him in the same soft voice she'd used the first time she told him she loved him. He suffered more from hearing that secret than he had when he'd learned she was dead, and he was convinced the dream was real.

In his dream, Yujin was the first to broach the subject, but she was the one who confessed, her face devoid of expression as she told him that she had been pregnant with his baby but got rid of it. Her voice was so flat, so lacking in any kind of emotion, that he wondered at first if she wasn't talking about someone else. He had never wanted a child, not while they were married and not after. Their divorce left him feeling relieved that they hadn't had one, but he also believed things would have turned out differently if they had. He didn't want to know what she was thinking or why she'd made that decision. He assumed the only reason she did it without consulting him was so she could leave him for Yujin, and that made him unbearably angry. He hurled invectives at her. But he didn't know if what really upset him was the fact that she'd had an abortion at all, or that she hadn't consulted him first, or if he was sad that his child was gone, or if it was none of the above and he'd simply found an excuse to unleash his anger.

Yujin looked back and forth between the two of them as if silently relishing the moment. In an attempt to rattle him, the man asked if Yujin knew that she had been cheating on Yujin with him. He hadn't sleep with his ex-wife solely to satisfy a physical desire. Just as when they were married, the sex lacked passion. Touching her was like touching himself, but that easy familiarity was what he liked about it. They didn't have to deal with the awkwardness of not knowing each other's bodies, or exaggerate their pleasure to avoid hurting each other's feelings. He never once assumed that his wife slept with him because she was unsatisfied in bed with Yujin. He just assumed that she too enjoyed lying beside him, staring up at the ceiling, glancing over at the side of his face from time to time, and talking.

Yujin countered by saying he already knew. This angered the man and made him lash out at Yujin only to get punched first. When his ex-wife tried to break up their fight, he shoved her by accident. The look on her face, a resigned expression that said fighting was pointless, incensed him further, and he went into the kitchen and grabbed a knife from the counter, intending only to anger her right back. He pointed it at Yujin. He was angry at his wife, but angrier still at Yujin for revealing her secret. Yujin's intentions were obvious: he wanted the man to suffer, just as the man wanted Yujin to suffer for breaking up his marriage. Amid the hazy unreality of it all, the feel of the knife in his hand, the glare he fixed on Yujin as he aimed the blade, and the regret when the knife clattered to the floor during their scuffle were so vivid that he would wake each time with a start.

He woke in the dark, the bench as hard as ever, his body slick with sweat. He could never tell if he was sweating from the nightmare or because the temperature in the park had risen from the decomposing trash. He would wait until the sky lightened enough for him to just make out the shape of his hand in the dark, then he would clench and release his fist over and over. The hand that had held the knife tingled and throbbed, and the stark chill he'd felt when he looked down at the fallen knife remained.

The sensation of holding a knife had seemed so concrete. He could picture every muscle and bone of that hand in detail. In fact, it was so overly vivid that it felt unreal. If he had indeed grabbed a knife while angry and confused, then his memories should have been distorted and jumbled, but he remembered it in perfect detail every time, as if it had been planted there in his mind. The sheer clarity of it made him convince himself that it was just a dream, nothing more than fancy. A mere fantasy generated by the fear that he might have killed his ex-wife.

The pain in his hand paled in comparison to remembering each time he awoke that his ex-wife was dead. He figured this was what dying of a broken heart would feel like. But the pain never lasted long. While he might freeze to death from lying on the ground in the rain, he knew he would never actually die of a broken heart. He kept living, no matter how badly his heart ached. He wished never to relive the past and yet, at least, back then, he was not being pelted with rain while lying on the bare earth, furrowing his brow as he tried to figure out whether that sensation creeping up his body and tickling his skin was from worms, the dampness, or the cold of the soil, or stifling a shriek each time he looked down to see fat drops of rain opening craters in the dirt and revealing the source to be worms after all.

In fact, he had to admit that the effort to endure his physical discomfort was inuring him to the pain of his ex-wife's death. Thinking about it still left him feeling beaten and raw, but even those pangs were growing shorter. The more often he grabbed the knife in his dreams, the less guilt he felt upon waking. Maybe the strange combination of the recurring nightmare with the vividness of the sensation was pushing his ex-wife's death into the realm of the unreal, the field of the imaginary. But even if it were a reality he would eventually have to face, even as he suffered over the loss of his ex-wife, he still had to crush the bugs that mistook his filthy, reeking body for a tree and climbed him, still had to run his fingers through hair turned muddy with sweat and rain and dirt and scratch until the undersides of his nails came away bloody, still had to flock with the other homeless men in the park at the sound of a passing dump truck and forage through garbage bags. He gladly put his grief second.

So much had happened in such a short time, but he did not know the truth of any of it. He gave up on understanding anything coming from himself. It could be that he did not want to understand, or that it was beyond his comprehension in the first place. But regardless of whether he understood, was resigned to, accepted, or misapprehended his ex-wife's death, he sensed that the suffering he had experienced so far was still better than the unforeseeable future making its way toward him. What depressed him was this: his current agony was nothing compared to what awaited him. All he could do was stay alive until he had put this world behind him.

* * *

He burst out laughing when he saw the street sign. Sixth Street, District 4. The park was a mere three blocks from his old apartment. The place he had thought of as far away wasn't far at all. How pathetic he was, calmly picking through the garbage, not knowing he had barely escaped. He had felt so at ease in the park because he believed he had put many miles between him and the apartment, and because he assumed the homeless were excluded from quarantining and therefore no cop or detective would bother searching the park.

He had clung to the top of the truck until his limbs hurt too much, certain that he'd held on long enough to at least reach another district. He couldn't believe that he'd only made it this far, and felt stupid for not figuring it out sooner. Each truck was assigned to one district, so naturally the one he had ridden had not left the neighborhood.

He headed toward his old building. It didn't take long to find, though he got lost along the way, crossing a few wrong streets and heading down a different alley. The building was as he remembered: it appeared to be floating on a cloud of disinfectant. But the riot police were gone. Either the quarantine had been lifted or the illness had spread out of control, leaving them with no reason to continue imposing the quarantine.

He peered through the glass doors that he could not enter. The superintendent, still dressed in a puffy hazmat suit, looked back at him with suspicion. The mask covering the superintendent's face made it impossible to tell if it was the same person as before.

The small park adjacent to the apartment, the one he used to look down at from his balcony, was not that different from the one he'd taken up residence in. Similarly unbathed vagrants were lying on benches, and the ground was also littered with garbage dragged over from the nearby garbage fire, making the whole place look like an upended trashcan.

And yet, the moment he entered the park, he felt that he had reached a peaceful and longed-for place. He thought maybe it was because of the phone booth, which was as brightly illuminated as a street lamp. Just the sight of it made him think of several people he missed, but the booth was packed with trash and the telephone itself was gone. He wished he could call someone that instant. Yujin, who had informed him of his ex-wife's death. Soyo, who hated him as much as Yujin did. His dead ex-wife. The more he longed to talk to someone, the more he realized that he had no one whom he could tell about his new surroundings, this world of garbage and germs. Then it hit him. Without a moment's hesitation, he headed off to find that person.

The sky was so dark that the office building had most of its lights ablaze even at midday. From a distance, he could see people on the other side of the large picture windows moving back and forth, sitting at their desks, busily engaged in meetings. He knew from this that everything was business as usual at company headquarters.

This attempt to meet Mol could very well end badly. Mol might have been the one who tipped off the men he had assumed were detectives. But he wanted to know whether or not he had ruined an otherwise serene future with a momentary lapse. He'd been thinking that maybe his leap into the garbage was a mistake born of a fleeting delusion. The thought began as a simple hope but had gradually turned into the conviction that it was all just a misunderstanding. A misunderstanding meant an opportunity to get his life back; he could still correct the life that had fallen into garbage.

Despite the high ceiling and bright fluorescents, the lobby was so deserted that it reminded him of an abandoned, underground city. The immaculate building made him feel like one of the public ashtrays sitting out on the sidewalk. Though, strictly speaking, they were cleaner than he was. A security guard stopped him the moment he stepped into the lobby. He felt indescribably filthy compared to the guard in his pristine hazmat suit. The guard had an electronic thermometer sticking out of his pocket: it seemed that permission to enter the building was based on body temperature, but the guard didn't bother with it; he took one look at the man and spread both arms out to stop him from entering. The man hurriedly said he was there to see Mol and recited Mol's job title and department to the guard, who was clearly intent on throwing him out on the street like a panhandler.

"You're asking to talk to one of our employees face to face?" The guard scowled, but then led him to a counter on the right side of the lobby and half-heartedly retrieved a blank form from a shelf labeled MEETING REQUEST FORMS. The man hadn't realized he would have to fill out a form just to be able to see Mol. It would not have stopped him from coming, of course, but he was stupefied by all the boxes he had to fill out.

"What happens if I don't fill this out?" he asked.

"You're a foreigner?" The guard sounded incredulous. The man slowly nodded. "Do you know how to write? We don't accept verbal requests for meetings."

Without waiting for an answer, the guard strode away, as if to say he was done helping him, and escorted out a group of people in black suits with masks over their noses and mouths who had just stepped off the elevator. The man stared hard at them. Some headed straight out the front door, while others hung back to wait for someone. He thought one of them might be Mol, whom he had yet to meet in person, and he scanned the ID cards hanging in plain sight on their chests. To his surprise, one of the cards did say Mol, but it was a woman. He didn't let that get him down. He had heard that Mol was a common name in that country.

He filled out each item on the form in his clumsy handwriting. When he got to "purpose of visit," he hesitated and looked over at the guard. He was taken aback to see the guard staring back at him. Since he already felt like a child waiting for a teacher to help show him the way, he wrote down "career guidance." He knew it wasn't quite right, but nothing better came to mind, and even if something had, he was not confident he would know how to say it in the local language anyway.

The guard pored over his application before finally saying, "*Career guidance*—that's a new one."

"Do you think I'll be granted a meeting?"

"I have no idea." The guard shrugged. "Sounds like something a high school student would write."

The man suspected the guard was making fun of him, and this made him feel like he'd made yet another mistake, but he summoned up his courage and asked, "When will I know?"

"I'm only responsible for sending these up to the office. Whoever is in charge there reviews the applications. If they okay it, then they pass it on to the person you wish to see. Do you understand? If they say no, your application is automatically thrown out. That's all I know. As with anything else, it takes a while for them to process these, so I cannot give you an exact time frame. Not everything is so precise. Do you understand?"

The guard gave him an indifferent look that said, yes, he had asked that question but, no, he did not actually care whether the man understood or not, and with a slow, dramatic flourish, he pulled open a drawer and set the man's application on top of a stack of dozens of other such submitted meeting request forms. Then he turned to face the door, as if to say his work here was done, and stood with his feet exactly hip-width apart and his hands behind his back. His posture, so like a soldier standing at ease, combined with the puffy suit reminded the man of the mascot of a foreign tire manufacturer, but there was nothing comical about it. Or maybe he just wasn't in a laughing mood. His determination to find Mol had left him feeling tragic.

He started to leave but paused to ask the guard another question.

"Can anyone fill out a form to see someone who works here?"

"Yes, anyone," the guard muttered, barely moving his lips.

"Including a cop or a detective?"

"Well, they only have to show their badge or a warrant. But they're not allowed inside if they're sick—they have to pass physical inspection, just like everyone else. Do you understand?"

"Do you think my application will be approved?"

The guard looked him over slowly, never once breaking his rigid stance even while turning his head.

"Like I said before, it's not up to me. So I don't know what to tell you. You shouldn't be swayed by my opinion. I don't want to get your hopes up too high or worry you over nothing. I'm just one man employed by the state. Do you understand?"

As the man turned again to leave, a group of people entered the lobby and lined up in front of the guard. The guard took the electronic thermometer from his pocket and checked each person's temperature and ID card in turn before letting them pass. The man watched until the lobby had emptied, and then he left. He would probably have his own temperature taken when he went back to check on the results of his application, so he knew he had better wash up and clean his clothes, but his steps grew heavy at the realization that getting dirtier by the day was so easy while getting clean was all but impossible. He would have to come back and see the same guard, and each time he did, he would have to give the same explanation over and over. The guard would tell him his application was still under review, and he would ask the same litany of questions to try to find out how much closer they were to deciding.

A few blocks away from the office, he came across a pile of trash bags lined up like a row of barracks between two buildings. He headed over to it happily. The wall of garbage had collapsed in places, but it didn't look like the sanitation workers had touched it yet. Several vagrants, a dog, and some stray cats were digging through the trash. He joined them, using one of the bags as a seat while he randomly opened up more bags and rummaged through the trash that had been strewn carelessly about or had burst out of other bags.

If it weren't for the other homeless men lying in the street like litter or passing the time by foraging through the trash, or for the giant banner overhead proclaiming how they could prevent the spread of infectious diseases, he would have felt like a tourist. The air was relatively fresh from the rain that had fallen the day before, and the fumigant had turned everything misty and made him feel like he was sitting on the bank of a fog-covered lake. The sprayer trucks had been coming by less frequently than usual. One should have passed by several times already, but the road was quiet. The clouds were lifting. For once, the air was clear. It felt like the first sunny day after the long summer rains. Though it would not last, it was the perfect weather for hoping that maybe the need for all of this control and prevention had finally come to an end.

As he was pulling a damp scrap of fabric from the trash, he spotted a familiar-looking suitcase. He couldn't tell it was a suitcase at first. With its wheels broken off, the suitcase itself was little more than a trash can giving off all sorts of smells. He slowly emptied the case. Out came a dried-up piece of meat infested with maggots—it looked like the corpse of some long-dead animal. The maggots crawled off of the meat and onto his hand, their bodies accordioning in little regular movements. He wasn't taken aback but simply brushed them off like they were so much dirt. A plastic bag filled with festering fruits and vegetables emerged next. With no time to adjust to the sudden blast of rot, he gagged. He moved to toss it to one side, and a stream of black discharge spilled onto the suitcase. Instantly, a swarm of flies descended as if they had been lying in wait. He reached back into the suitcase and pulled out part of a broken bowl, its original use now unknowable, and long-unwashed clothes that smelled like dishrags. He dumped it all on the ground and examined the case.

It was an ordinary black suitcase, so common that it would be easily confused with another person's suitcase at baggage claim. But the handle would prove whether or not it was his bag. The original plastic handle of his suitcase had broken off while it was still under warranty, and the company had replaced it with a new, imitation-leather handle, attached on each side with white stitching. He lifted up the bag and took a long, careful look at the handle. One end had come undone and the rest was barely hanging on, but the handle was indeed sewn to the case—the thread was too dirty to make out the original color, but he was sure it had once been white.

Maggots from the long-dead animal were crawling along the suitcase, looking like stray bits of white thread. He unzipped the front pocket. It was stuffed with objects he didn't recognize. A smaller pocket inside the suitcase refused to open. The zipper was rusted shut. It stayed shut no matter how hard he tugged. Once, on the way back from a business trip, he had packed a can of local beer inside his suitcase: the can exploded from the change in pressure, and the zipper had rusted. Since he had never gotten the zipper open again, whatever he had packed inside that pocket would still be there.

He took out his knife. He rested the dull blade against the fabric and scraped it back and forth across the same spot. His heart raced as he pictured what might be inside. Finding his lost suitcase after all that time was no small matter. This trash can of a suitcase might still hold something that he had brought with him from his mother country. Whatever was inside that pocket might even cast some much-needed light on his situation. It could restore his memories, which felt like mere dreams to him now, or prove vital to clearing himself of these false charges, or even play a role in identifying the real criminal. He took his time, running the knife back and forth, back and forth, over the same spot until the fabric began to split. He inserted the tip of the knife into the tiny slit he'd created and ran the blade along the grain, tearing a long hole down the side of the pocket. Just as he'd hoped, there was something inside. All he had to do now was pull it out. He hesitated for the briefest of moments and slowly slipped his fingers in.

He felt something hard and rough. It felt exactly like the wiry fur of a monkey's tail that he had touched once long ago. When he saw what he pulled out, he fell back. It was a rat, long dead and as hard as a fossil. The suitcase pocket that he'd thought might harbor a secret had already been ransacked, and the rat that had mistakenly crawled in had been trapped there by someone, and left to stiffen like plaster.

The park was as silent as a dead mouse. So quiet that he could hear the other vagrants' exhalations. But the stillness was mixed with a rustling and a quiet stirring. He listened closer. Someone was struggling to inhale through congested sinuses and exhale through a clogged windpipe. It was clearly more labored than anyone else's breathing. As he turned his head left and right, trying to catch where the sound was coming from, someone tapped him on the shoulder. He had been so engrossed in the strange breathing that he'd failed to notice the sound of footsteps drawing near. He turned to look, thinking as he did so that if there was one thing more frightening then infectious disease, it was an unexpected visit, like this one. There was nothing to be done about disease other than wait for death, but surprise visitors rarely brought anything good. He couldn't accept the thought of possibly losing his bench. All that work just to find somewhere he could stretch out and rest, and now to have it taken from him, this splintery old wooden bench that he would guard as fiercely as if it were a home he had lived in his whole life, no, he would fight for it, would bleed and break bones for it, and probably, in the end, lose it.

Chin quivering, he turned, barely able to meet the eyes of the man standing behind him. The man's face was hidden behind a scraggly beard, and his hair had grown down to his shoulders and was matted like straw. His clothes gave off an odd smell, mixed with the stench of urine. They were dirtied and stained from being soaked with rain and drying, then soaked with sweat and drying, over and over. Steam rose from the other man's body like a heat shimmer. Judging from the acrid smell, the man had pissed his pants, either moments before or while walking over to him.

Number Eight had come to the park after him. That was back when the man was able to find a bench without having to fight for it. Eight had arrived dressed in a dark suit and white button-down shirt. He had stood for a long time, gazing up at the sky and around at the park, hazy as usual with disinfectant, before taking his messenger bag off of his shoulder, removing a book from it, and sitting down on the eighth bench to read. At first, he looked like he was only there to pass the time before his next appointment, but when night fell, he lay down in the same spot and fell asleep, and the next morning he awoke early and resumed reading. The man assumed Eight was the victim of an untimely "honorary retirement" and had left his house that morning as if going to work as usual only to find himself with nowhere to go. Eight remained in the park as his white shirt turned less and less white and his beard grew with abandon and slowly hid his face. The vagrants in the park rarely poked their noses into each other's business, but someone finally let his curiosity get the better of him—probably Three or Six, who were prone to chattiness—and asked how he had ended up there. Eight hesitated and then said he'd been kicked out of his company. When the other person pried a little more, he admitted that he had been fired because his employers thought he was infected. At that, his inquisitor jumped back in alarm.

"I'm still alive," Eight said with a laugh. "That's proof enough that I'm not infected."

But no one went near him again after that.

While the others were busy digging through the trash for food that was hardly better than trash, cramming their mouths no matter how rotten the food was just to ensure it wasn't stolen from them first, Eight sat calmly and sipped only enough water to keep his throat from drying out and closing up, as if to prove to them all that he was not sick. Of course, as the days passed, Eight gradually spent less time reading his book and more time rummaging through garbage, but even then he moved slowly, picking through items deliberately like he was shopping in a supermarket, as if only interested in finding whatever was absolutely necessary, rather than lunging at others like a starving ghost to keep their hands off of his things. He was able to take his time like this, because no one else would go near him.

"You hear that?"

The man looked in the direction of the sound to show that he did.

"Something needs to be done about it," Eight continued.

He heard Eight say something else that sounded like "if we don't get rid," but he couldn't make out the next words. Eight's voice was too low, and he kept glancing around uneasily and avoiding the man's eyes, which made it impossible to read his lips. But he was able to guess the part he'd missed: if they didn't get rid of the sick man, they would get sick too, and if that happened they were all dead.

"He's coughing up blood. And gagging. His face is red from fever." Eight held up his book, the words spilling out in a rush. "I learned all about it from this. Fever is the first sign. I had a fever too. The lymph nodes in your armpits, groin, and throat swell, and your temperature goes way up. But that didn't happen to me. It says that if the pathogens invade your nervous system, you slip in and out of consciousness and start to hallucinate. Toward the end, you vomit blood, your body leaks pus, and you convulse. Then you die. They say the virus is highly contagious and spreads through the air like pollen."

The man quietly took a step back, preferring not to stand too close to Eight. Nor was he interested in Eight's declaration that he was not sick.

"So anyone who catches it dies fast," said one of the other vagrants, who had stolen over at some point. The man wasn't sure, but he thought it might be Five. The others in the park, who ordinarily guarded their benches in silence, began to gather around them.

"That's right," said Eight. "From fever to death, just like that! But if you survive, like me, then that shows you only had a cold." He sounded proud of himself.

"If those are the symptoms, does that mean we've all been infected?" muttered someone who might have been Seven. "That's impossible."

"No way I'm infected," said someone he assumed was Ten. "He's the only one. I'm not going to die."

"I wish I were infected. Then I wouldn't be knocking my brains out with worry over getting infected," said Seven.

"If that's really your wish, then go stand next to him," said Eight.

Seven flinched and took a step back. Everyone turned to look at where Two was lying. Two must have been concealing his fever and nausea for some time, conscious of the other vagrants around him. If the skin beneath his filthy clothes had turned red and inflamed, then it was already too late. It was said that, in the final stages of this contagion, your blood burst through the capillary walls and turned your skin dark and bruised.

While running a high fever, Two would have hurried to where the garbage was burned, and shoved and punched the other men to try to lay claim to the few scraps of food mixed in with the refuse. He would have had coughing fits that sent his spit flying through the air and, when winded, he would have leaned against whichever bench was closest to him, propping up his tired body with the same hands he had used to wipe away his spit. If anyone else in that park got sick, it would be Two's fault.

Two let out a long breath and trembled violently. According to Eight, the infected in the final stage of the illness would tear out their own hair, unable to bear even the mild pain brought on by the boils on their bodies. Their pulses would race, and then gradually slow, and then become thready and faint just before death took them.

"But the good thing," Eight said, "is that the pain doesn't last too long. If there's one blessing to this particular disease, it's that it helps you meet your end quickly."

The group slunk toward Two with Eight in the lead. Not one of them offered that maybe Two just had a bad cold or that, even if he was infected, maybe they were going too far. Fear of contagion crowded out sympathy. They were already living like trash, but the disease was fatal, in that it took away their ability to choose between life and death. Not that they aspired to a great life. They simply feared death. Of course, it could be just a cold, nothing more than a simple fever, but it didn't matter. This was the age of epidemics. You couldn't be too careful. The fact that the routes of contagion were uncertain meant that you could catch the virus from the air or from a simple brush of skin. Disease to a vagrant meant certain death. If one of them was sick, then any of them could become sick. Therefore, anyone who was sick or was suspected of being sick had to leave the park, and if they did not leave voluntarily, or if they could not leave, then it stood to logic that they must be gotten rid of.

While crossing the park, the man realized for the first time that the trees at the center were called camphor trees and that they normally had lush green leaves on branches that spread wide in all directions. Because of the fumigation, the leaves had withered black or dried to a yellowish brown and fallen, but new, pale green leaves were already sprouting. Each time the wind blew, the trees shook their branches as if to rid themselves of the lingering chemical haze.

As they drew closer, the man saw Two's long, matted hair, the untrimmed beard, the face blackened with dirt, and the filthy clothes and was taken aback by how much he resembled him. The only difference was that Two was sick while he was not yet sick. The realization broke his stride, but then he saw that he was noticeably lagging and picked up his pace.

The clothes he wore had been picked out of the trash a few days earlier. He and Two, along with several of the other park vagrants, were wearing identically colored shirts with different names stitched on the front. A large garbage bag had held random fabric scraps along with a stack of shirts that seemed to be part of some team or group uniform: they had matching images on the front with the names of their intended owners stitched over the heart in gold thread. There were enough that the men could choose the size and name they wanted; he had chosen one stitched with the name MOL, realizing all over again how common the name was in that country.

Two struggled to open his eyes. He must have heard them coming, or maybe he had finally gained control of the pain in his lungs. He had boils on his face, and blood and pus dripped like sweat from his forearm. Symptoms had taken up residence in his body, but whether they heralded deadly contagion or just a run-of-the-mill skin condition was unknowable. Eight approached Two and asked how he was feeling. His voice sounded friendly and considerate. It bore no trace of malice. Two made an effort to smile and nodded slowly. He started to say something, but he never got the chance. Before he could get a single word out, Eight threw a body bag over him. There had been rumors of corpses wrapped in body bags showing up in the dump. Some said the morgues were discarding unidentified bodies, and others said they were the corpses of the infected that the hospitals could not accommodate. Despite all the talk, the man himself had yet to see an actual body.

Instead of the words he was going to say, Two let out a scream that was closer to a groan. But that was as far as he got. He was already zipped into the bag. His breathing grew rougher. He writhed in desperation like a trapped bug. The body bag clung to his face with each inhale and ballooned out with each exhale. If they left him in there long enough, he would suffocate before the disease took him.

The man had been keeping his distance, but someone shoved him forward. Defenseless, he stumbled and fell to his knees next to the bag. Three others were volunteered the same way.

"Pick it up."

The order came from someone with a low voice. Surprisingly firm, the voice brooked no disobedience. Their reluctance wasn't because they didn't want to harm the ailing man, it was simply fear of touching the infected. As they hesitated, a sprayer truck passed by. An enormous chemical cloud surged through the park and hid the men from each other. This somehow made it easier for them to hoist Two onto their shoulders. Two groaned and struggled.

They had just begun to move toward the garbage fire when something grabbed the man's arm. It was Two. He had wiggled the zipper open and slipped his hand out. His grip was strong, but what filled the man with horror was the damp, tacky feeling of Two's palm. He pictured blood and pus. This, he thought, is what it would feel like to get sucked into a swamp. He flinched and shoved Two's hand off of his arm. The other three men carrying the body bag jerked their hands away for fear of being touched. Two hit the ground with a loud moan and rolled back and forth, still wrapped in the bag. The man pulled his foot back and kicked Two, over and over.

"Pick it up."

They were the first words he'd spoken aloud in the park. The other three looked cowed by his bullying tone and awkwardly lifted Two to their shoulders again.

They heard a car not far off. It was the small car driven by the government employee in charge of minding the trash fire. By now, they were all adept at telling from the sound of the engine alone whether it was a sprayer truck, a garbage truck, or the employee's car. With Two slung over their shoulders again, they started to move. They had to hurry. If there was a best time for throwing garbage on the fire, that time was now.

The fire had been rekindled: a white haze of smoke was beginning to billow. Soon, red flames would flicker, and black smoke would mix with the white and climb above the fire. To keep Two from working his way out of the bag and coming after them in retaliation, the men rushed over to where the garbage was burned and waited until the flames were high and crackling, keeping a firm grip on the bag as Two writhed desperately, and then got as close as they could before throwing him onto the pyre. There was an audible thump, but it was nearly lost in the sounds of trash burning. As they walked away, the man thought he heard a scream. It sounded a little like someone crying for help. The yells faded into a pained groan. But it was just an auditory hallucination. By the time they returned to their benches, the only sound echoing around them was of garbage burning. Along with the sound, a cloud of black smoke crept through the park.

Someone coughed. More coughs burst out here and there, as if they had all been holding them in. The smoke was making them cough. The man knew that it took about an hour and a half to cremate an adult male. For the hour and a half that Two would burn, his smoke would billow up and fill the air. He had never seen Two's face. Had never spoken to him. But there he was, breathing him in.

He reassured himself that it had not been his idea to get rid of Two. He was not the one who had thrown the body bag over him. He was not the first to give the order to pick him up. All he had done was be pushed by someone, and when he was overcome with fear at being grabbed by Two's blood and pus-covered hand, had kicked him, and merely to overcome that fear, picked Two up again and ran with him to the trash fire.

He knew he was afraid because he could hear his own heartbeat. This was not some moral twinge. Two had grabbed his arm hard, and now, for all he knew, he too would soon be overcome by fever and erupt in red sores bursting with pus. He wished he could chop off the arm that Two had touched.

He flexed every muscle and willed every hole in his body to open. He let his jaw gape to allow the saliva to flow out, and he took deep gulps of the fumigant and the black smoke from the garbage fire that were floating in the air. The smoke was dark and burned his lungs, but it wasn't much worse than any other day. He coughed until he thought his intestines were coming out of his mouth. His eyes welled with tears. The trash took longer to burn than usual. The embers glowed for a long time, illuminating the night, and the ash, lighter than air, floated about the park like souls until the sun came up.

He awoke from a deep sleep to see legs surrounding him in the haze. He couldn't make them out clearly. There were a lot of them, looking like they were out for a stroll in the park, their torsos lost in the chemical fog. But you could never be too careful. He stifled a cough and tried to stand, a slight ache lighting up different areas of his body. When he thought he was fully upright, he found himself being forced back down again. A hand pressed hard on his shoulder. His body tensed. Frightened, he opened his eyes wider, but something covered his face, and he couldn't see. All at once, he realized he'd been stuffed into a body bag just like Two. Each time he opened his mouth to breathe, the fabric suctioned to his face. He felt his body rise into the air. He squirmed inside the sack. As he struggled, his opaque future turned transparent. He was about to be tossed into darkness.

TWO

He and his ex-wife went to the tropics once. It was the first trip they had taken together since their honeymoon. And though he did not know it at the time, it would turn out to be their last. They had tried taking other trips together, but their plans fell apart each time. He'd assumed that this trip, too, would come to nothing, but his ex-wife had surprised him by putting her foot down. He told her he couldn't take time off of work, and rather than accept his answer as she ordinarily would have, she declared she would go alone. In retrospect, that might have been when she'd sensed that his suspicions of her were taking over. And so, under the glaring eyes of Trout and his other coworkers, he requested time off and accompanied his wife. He took the risk of missing work because he figured this trip might be his last chance to repair his marriage.

It didn't have to be that country, but there weren't many options that fit their travel dates and could be booked last minute. Besides, neither of them actually cared where they went. They booked a guided tour, just as they had on their honeymoon. Though traveling with a guide meant being hustled along from site to site, as if each place were merely another item to be checked off a list, and herded into over-sized tourist shopping centers where they would endure long sales pitches for latex foam bedding, sapphires, rubies, medicinal mushrooms, and other local goods sold by immigrants and have no choice but to buy those shoddy products at inflated prices just to keep their guide happy, it was still better than the awkwardness of being on their own all day with no itinerary at all. As it turned out, they were the only ones on the group tour.

Not only were they in the subtropics, it was the rainy season and the humidity was high. It was so hot that they had to keep fanning away the sweat even inside the air-conditioned van. When he wouldn't stop grumbling about the heat, the guide jokingly scolded him and asked why, then, had he decided to come there in the hot summer.

"Hot summer? Isn't it always hot summer here?"

"We have two seasons: summer and hot summer."

The guide spoke a simplified version of their language. His wife tittered.

"Some say three seasons," the guide added. "Summer, hot summer, and really hot summer."

His wife laughed and asked, "Then which season is this?"

"Really hot summer."

As it turned out, they were traveling right in between the

ultimately indistinguishable seasons of hot summer and really hot summer. The weather would go from boiling hot to rain coming down in buckets, and after a while the sun would beat down again until their rain-soaked clothes gave off steam. He didn't know if it was the unpredictable weather or the annoying way in which his wife kept staring off into space, lost in thought, her face stony, but his mood turned prickly and he became stubborn about every little thing.

It was the same in the monkey forest. On the last day of their trip, right around noon, the rain started drumming down, as loud as hailstones, so the guide suggested they skip elephant trekking and sightsee downtown instead. His wife readily agreed. But he pulled a face and told the guide exactly how sick and tired he was of being dragged around to tourist traps and asked if there wasn't some quiet, secluded spot where the locals went. He was planning to use just such a spot to talk to his wife. They had been sticking to the itinerary, rushing from place to place and returning to their hotel room at night only to exaggerate how exhausted they were in order to go right to sleep. Already they were scheduled to return home the next day. If they wasted another half day shopping, he would lose the opportunity to tell her how he really felt, and to make her tell him how she felt.

"Quiet place? Like a temple?" the guide asked.

"Temples are okay, but that last one you took us to was overrun with tourists. I don't want to go there. I want some place that isn't well known, something off the beaten path."

"Go north a hundred and fifty kilometers, there's a forest temple. Lots of monkeys, hardly any people. Good?"

His wife wrinkled her nose at the word *monkeys*.

"How deserted is this place?" she asked.

"Very. No one knows it. Lots of monkeys. It's called Monkey Forest."

"Can you imagine how many monkeys there must be for it to be called that? That sounds scary. Let's go somewhere else," she said firmly.

"What's so scary about monkeys?" the man said. "People go there, too. I bet the monkeys are more afraid of the people."

He told the guide to take them there.

His wife stared out the window and did not say a word during the whole two-hour drive. He kept glancing over at the side of her face and inwardly regretting his stubbornness, while at the same time feeling such despair that he wished the van would get there faster so that he and his wife would finally have some time to themselves.

The guide let them off at the entrance to the dense forest without much in the way of instructions. As they stepped out of the van, he heard a flock of birds in the distance. Only later, when they were inside the forest, did he realize those weren't birdcalls but rather the screeching of monkeys.

They had just stepped into the shadow of the trees when the guide, who had told them he would wait for them in the van, called them back.

"Lots of monkeys. Scary. Understand?"

"I can't do this," his wife said. "Let's just go."

She gave him a look that said she meant it. But he avoided her eyes and said, "You don't really think you're going to be killed by a monkey, do you?"

He stepped back into the forest. Whether resigned or simply too angry to argue with him, his wife followed.

They had not gone far when he realized that this dense, dark forest filled with towering trees that blocked out the sky should have been called a jungle. The trees were as tightly packed as the air itself, and outnumbering the trees were the monkeys hopping from branch to branch and harassing who or whatever wandered in. There wasn't a single other soul in sight. The guide had followed the man's request exactly and brought them to a quiet, secluded spot. Later, after they'd made it out of the forest, he realized that the monkeys were the same species as those he had seen in zoos back home, but in the moment he could not properly make out the shapes of the countless bodies that confronted him and his wife as they made their way to the temple.

The temple sat at the center of the forest, which was shaped like a deep *U;* there was no way to get from end to end without passing the temple. Other than the path, a mere line of trampled grass, everything else was covered in tall trees and dense undergrowth. The heavy shade of the tangled trees, the calling of unseen birds that filled the air, the queer screeching of monkeys that immediately followed as if in response to the birdcall, the eerie sound of wind rattling the leaves, and the cold, damp air wafting up from the ground made their teeth chatter.

"Well, I guess we know their god is male. Why else would they build a temple somewhere this dark and wet? Am I right?"

He only made the joke as an excuse to get them talking, but his wife strode on ahead and didn't respond. She usually scoffed at his failed jokes. In the silence that followed, he sensed that, since entering this dark forest that could care less about them, he and his wife had been slowly leaving the world in which their lives overlapped. The feeling made him want to pull his wife, who was now several paces ahead of him, back by his side and keep her there, but he never got the chance. She screamed. A black object had wrapped itself around her face. He ran to her, but the object suddenly vanished, as if nothing more than a shadow. His wife's sunglasses had vanished with it. A monkey. Terrified, his wife clung to his side. She clutched his forearm, but he could tell it held no more meaning than an elderly person leaning on a cane. Still, he knew he would not soon forget the heat flowing from his wife's hand to his arm.

That was the beginning. Their path to the temple was a progression of lost objects. The next monkey snatched his wife's hat. That too happened in the blink of an eye. The man chased after the monkey to try to retrieve the hat. He spotted one or two other people in the distance, but they were locals, and it wasn't clear whether they were just visiting or actually lived in the forest. They watched as he chased after the monkey, their faces suggesting that this was something they saw all the time and yet found as entertaining as ever. They looked serene, as if they had nothing the monkeys could take from them, or perhaps nothing left to be taken.

The man gave up on chasing the animal down. It had scrambled up a tall tree and disappeared into the forest. He could have followed it into the trees, but then he would have stumbled across an entire troop or gotten lost in the dense, shady woods.

As he was walking back to his wife, panting and trying to catch his breath, two monkeys jumped him at the same time. He threw his arms out to the side, breathing in the foul smell, the stink of urine, and something else that reminded him of wet grass coming off of the monkey wrapped around his face. He managed to pull them off of him, but his hat and sunglasses were now gone, and he had several scratches, both deep and shallow.

He immediately regretted the decision to come there and tried to turn around. But the way back was so dark and thick with trees that he and his wife could not locate the entrance. They had no choice but to keep going until they reached the temple. They walked and walked, but there were only more trees and no temple in sight. The path seemed to lead only to deeper jungle. The farther they went, the more monkeys they encountered, and each time, they lost another of their belongings. Sometimes the monkeys emerged only to tease and anger them: one would abruptly drop from a branch right in front to scare them, or burst out of the forest and grab his wife's ankle to make her fall, or smack the back of the man's head with its tail and run off again into the trees, too fast to be caught.

Just as the round roof of the temple was coming into view among the treetops and they were breathing a sigh of relief, two more monkeys attacked. They bit his arms, clawed at his eyes, and let out a bloodcurdling shriek as they took the black bag he had been clutching to his chest as if it were his heart itself. The bag contained his passport and wallet. He had pretended not to hear his wife when she had urged him to leave them in the hotel safe. Lately, the more right she was, the less he listened. Despite his frantic efforts, the two monkeys would not leave him alone. His bag was quickly stolen. He ran after the monkey with his bag around its neck and grabbed its long tail as it was about to leap into a tree. He pulled hard and sank his teeth into the wiry fur. It felt like an enormous caterpillar squirming inside his mouth. He clenched his jaw as hard as he could, his eyes shut tight, teeth bearing down through the tough, foul-smelling skin and tender bones. A crunching sound pealed inside his head. He thought he would never forget that sound for as long as he lived. The feel of those wiry hairs, the crumbling of bone, the sticky saliva trailing from his open mouth. He would not forget those things.

The monkey's hair stood on end and it let out a piercing scream. He held it down with one arm and fumbled with the

CITY OF ASH AND RED

other until his hand fell on a long, heavy fallen branch. He jabbed the tip of the branch at the monkey's back, but it glanced off. Nothing was ever easy. Taking a firmer grip on the tail, he stabbed the monkey over and over with the branch as it screamed and struggled to free itself. Some of the blows landed on the monkey while others struck his own forearm that held the monkey in place, and some of the blows hit nothing at all. When the stick missed the monkey and pierced his thigh instead, he thought he might drop dead from the pain, but he didn't care. He would kill himself if that was what it took to kill the monkey. Screams—were they his wife's screams as she finally caught up to him? the monkey's screams? his own?—slipped under and over the dark tangle of branches overhead and echoed deep into the forest.

He did not let go until the animal lay slumped and weakened. But the moment he released his grip, the monkey that had seemed as good as dead suddenly sprang up and leapt into the trees without a look back. He watched as its red bottom disappeared among the branches. His body ached. His forearm and thigh were throbbing. He wasn't sure, but he might have even broken a bone. A thorn on the branch must have opened a vein, because the wound in his thigh bled profusely and soaked his pant leg. Fat drops of rain began to splatter down from the dark sky, as if to scold him.

His bag was gone, snatched up by the other monkey while he was busy fighting. Only after he had lost everything did he realize that what he had fought so desperately to save amounted to nothing. Other than his wife, he didn't want anything badly enough to resort to biting a monkey's tail and stabbing himself in the arm and thigh.

He got angry at her because of that. He got angry because, here he was, covered in blood, and still he knew he could not keep her. Just as he had failed to keep his passport and wallet, he was incapable of keeping her no matter how great the wounds he suffered. And not only that, all of this had been his choice alone. What if his wife were the one who had insisted they go to the temple? What if she had told him to chase down a thieving monkey to get her money and passport back? And what if she had persuaded him to stab the monkey over and over? Then he would not have had to take up that branch and attack the monkey until he was covered in his own blood with no clue as to what he was trying to hold on to.

On their way out of the forest, the monkeys left them alone since they had nothing left to take, and so he unleashed his fury on his wife instead. His wife took his baseless accusations in silence, as if he were talking about someone else, and her silence made him even angrier. He had to clamp down hard on the urge to beat her. If he hadn't injured his arm, if he could have lifted his arm or used it at all, he might not have been able to hold back.

Later, when he recalled the events at the temple, he felt shocked at his own unfamiliar self. Grabbing a tree branch, which he'd never before regarded as a weapon, to stab a monkey to death, and gladly enduring his own injuries in the process? Confessing his paranoid suspicions and accusing his wife of being a two-timing whore just to soothe his own anger, and disparaging her sexually by unleashing bad words he hadn't used since he was a teenager? Knowing he would have hit her if he'd had any strength left? It all kept him feeling ashamed of himself for a long time after.

When they returned from the temple, his wife bought bandages and medicine and helped patch him up, but the next morning she took her passport from the hotel safe and left for home. Their itinerary complete, the guide left as well to lead another group of tourists. The man had to go to the hospital on his own without knowing a single word of the language, get his passport reissued from the embassy, and wait for his wife to wire him money for the rest of his travel expenses, hating himself all the while.

After that trip, every time anger rose up in him, he pictured spidery limbs wrapped around his face, monkeys hanging brazenly from his body and blacking out his vision, giving off their odorous funk. Whenever he pictured it, his heart shivered like it was shrinking inside his chest and his head ached from the effort to bear the tremors, but what frightened him was not those horrible, marauding monkeys but rather the choices he had made when his back was to the wall.

* * *

He struggled to lift his eyelids, to try to dislodge the monkey stuck to his face. He was in a dark place filled with the shadows of trees. He was still there, still making his way through a forest of wild monkeys bent on looting him of everything he had. One of the monkeys, giving off a stink so vile that his stomach threatened to unload itself, slapped his right cheek, then his left. His eyes sprang open. He could not lose any more to them. If there was one good thing, it was that no matter how deep this forest was or how dark or how many thieving animals hid in its shadows, it would have to end eventually. And he knew when it would end. It would end when he had nothing more to lose. The monkey that had slapped him fell on its bottom in surprise. It grunted with displeasure and spat on the ground. Slowly the forest evaporated and a black ceiling appeared. The long-haired monkey looked him over. It grasped his wrist and lifted it into the air. The rest of his arm followed weakly, like a puppet dangling from strings, and fell back to the ground with a thump.

The monkey said something, but the man caught only one word: "still." He wasn't sure if that meant he was still alive, or still not dead. Coming and going before his addled eyes were the long, salt-and-pepper hair and scraggly, overgrown beard of an old man who looked and smelled as foul as a monkey.

As he lay there like a corpse, the old man turned him side to side to strip off his shirt. The shirt was not his to begin with, but it had fit the man perfectly and had the name MOL stitched on the front. It was much too large for the scrawny old man, but the old man didn't care.

The man remembered the knife in his pocket and gently groped the side of his pants. As he did so, he realized that his hand, the pants, his shoes, and his hair were soaked. He recalled floundering in midair before being tossed into cold water. The only source of running water near the park was the sewer tunnel that led to the river around the island. They must have resorted to that, since the fire would have burned out by then. They would not have wanted him coming to and rushing back to the park. His body ached in several places, as if he had hit something on the way down. Luckily, he still had the knife. He had a hunch that, though this knife had done nothing for him so far and he hoped it never would, it would eventually be the only thing that kept him safe. The moment would come in which his survival would depend on that single, blunt knife.

He tried to sit up but bumped his head hard against a low ceiling. He didn't know what it was at first and thought someone was shoving him back down. He thought about getting to his knees to beg his captor to spare his life, but then the old man spoke.

"Everyone does that at first. After a few days, your head will remember. It won't remember not to hit the ceiling, but it won't hurt as much."

The man leaned back and looked around. An intricate tangle of pipes of various sizes ran overhead. The pillars and ceiling were corroded, the concrete flaking and pitted, and the walls were damp with moss and looked slippery. Water leaking down from the ceiling ended in mud puddles. A step away from where he reclined, a river of sewage, black as petroleum, slipped past.

The old man put on the damp yellow shirt and shuffled on his knees farther into the shadows. The man sat forward, intending to follow him, but realized as he did so that he was injured. His right leg. He had hit it hard on something. He limped after the old man. The old man flinched at the sound of the leg dragging on the ground and paused. The old man probably thought he wanted his shirt back. To show the old man he meant no harm, he put on the shirt the old man had discarded. It was soiled and stinking and worn through in places, but he did not care.

When the old man saw that the man had no intention of stealing his shirt back, he moved slowly over to a spot beneath a large pipe. The sound of some enormous machinery in motion was coming from somewhere, but it was relatively warm and the smell there wasn't as bad. He plopped down next to the old man, who immediately began to snore. For all he knew, the old man might have been faking sleep in order to avoid talking to him.

The *drip-drip* of water was constant, and he could hear a screeching sound coming from somewhere deep inside the pipes, but the noise soon died down and felt no more real than a distant echo. The dense funk of rot was everywhere, but that too was not as bad as the pungent smell of the fumigants aboveground that had burned his nose.

Other than the intermittent stabs of pain in his leg, the night passed more or less comfortably. He could think of it as comfortable, despite lying in a sewer tunnel with an injured leg, because all cities had large sewer tunnels like this one, and as long as he was down there, he did not have to worry about being driven out. He could stay down there, free as he pleased, until his leg got better. As he realized the truth of this, he breathed easy, caught up in the pleasure of his hard-won freedom and believing that he would not be cast down into darkness a second time. But at the same time, he was forced to taste his own pessimism and humiliation for feeling so relieved at the thought that he had escaped violence and assault.

As the man sat and stared at the sewage flowing past, it occurred to him that he would probably have to enter those dark waters again, the same way he had drifted here from the park. The day might come when he would have to dip his body beneath its dark surface and escape to the opposite shore, or a moment arise in which he would be forced to drink that water to survive. Of course, that was not the case right now. But the moment was coming.

He wasn't worried. The future was far too distant a thing to worry about now, and the present was filled with survival. All he could afford to think about was the past. The future was unknowably vast and colossal and so very, very far away. The only thing he knew for sure about it was that it was a time that had not yet come. As he gazed into that water as black as petroleum, he understood that time never quite did what it was supposed to. Time sometimes got bogged down in the mud and sometimes mixed with raw sewage and slid sluggishly past. Which meant the future might never arrive at all.

Like an old man on his deathbed brooding over the days and hours of time gone by, he gazed into the black wastewater, preoccupied with conjuring up the past. The past that filled his head was all tackiness and triviality. Things that, at the moment of their happening, he would never have pegged for one day causing him to shudder with longing. A Chopin sonata that his ex-wife once played for him at the piano school on the last night of the year after all the students had gone home, the piano so out of tune that every note sounded like it was on the verge of tears. The motel where they'd had sex for the first time, and the blue-winged fan hanging from the ceiling that did nothing to cool their sweat. A Ferris wheel on the beach that creaked and swayed as they rode it, long after the season had ended. The front tooth he broke as a child when he tripped while running after his friends, and the sound of his mother's voice when she threw the tooth onto the roof of the house and sang for the birds to carry it off. As he looked up at the shafts of dusty light filtering through the edges of a manhole, he remembered sitting on a hardwood floor as the sunlight cast long shadows and his wife giggled. She was painting his toenails. They were too thick for him to feel those slow brushstrokes, but his wife's long hair had brushed the tops of his feet and tickled his skin each time she dipped her head. He later forgot all about his polished toes until he went to a sauna with the other men from his department and was mortified when they discovered it.

Now, in what felt like an eternity later, it all made him want to cry: The thought of that blue-winged fan that kept him wanting to embrace his wife despite how hot and close the room was. The sonata whose shivery notes delighted him each time his wife pressed another key. The broken tooth tossed onto the roof and carried away, though whether by a bird or a rat he had no idea. His red toenails. Not because he regretted having lived a life so basic and unappealing, but because he was cut off from those times, those hours spent in a reality filled with the trite and trivial. For all he knew, he would be forever distanced from them. This despair at knowing he would never make his way back weighed heavily on him. And he grew unhappy at the thought that he might never again run his fingers along the fine grain of ordinary everyday life.

Things that hid themselves in the dark of night were revealed in the hazy light seeping in from above. When that happened, the man saw bodies moving quietly, giving off a faint glow. At first glance he thought they were rats, but they were not. They were people. They were bigger than sewer rats but no better. They, too, moved through dark, dirty places as if right at home there. The sewer was as full of people as it was of rats. Most had been there since before the epidemic began. Just as most of the people he'd met in the park had already been homeless.

The sewer was dirtier than any other place he had ever been. The concrete walls and floor. The tangle of pipes overhead. The pillars. The metal ladders leading up to the ground. Everything was filthy. The air they breathed was filthy, and the breaths they exhaled were filthy, and most of all, *they* were filthy. Like vermin marking territory, some made living spaces for themselves out of discarded items they had found. Though it was dark and the ceiling too low for comfort, they managed something resembling bedrooms. They laid down mattresses scavenged from garbage dumps, dragged in discarded wardrobes and filled them with clothes they'd found in the trash. They placed large, warped washbasins wherever the rain leaked in and used the water to bathe, and they combed their hair while gazing into shards of broken mirrors fitted into the gaps between the pipes.

Meanwhile the man witnessed the others belching and pissing and shitting wherever they pleased. Most urinated into the black water or defecated next to where they sat. Some even went so far as to relieve themselves right where they lay, and simply rolled over to avoid the steaming puddle. He heard men masturbating, day or night, not caring at all that others watched. In fact, they were so blatant about watching that they even made fun of each other by timing how long it took them to climax. Fights broke out, but never lasted long since they all knew the tables could turn at any moment and the teaser would become the teased.

The old man sometimes muttered comments to him under his breath, but he seemed less to be hoping for a response than assuming he would not get one. At least, the man figured as much from the simple, pointless things he talked about: "That old guy, him, over there, the old guy with the red blanket, he's been here eight years, give or take, but I've never—look at that rotten bread he's got! It's blue with mold!—never once seen him get diarrhea, not even after he eats bread like that."

Though he knew the man never spoke, the old man asked him one day, "What should I call you? I might need a name for you at some point."

He stared back at the old man, as if incapable of speech. The old man's voice took on a nagging tone.

"I need to know your name if I'm going to share any of my food with you. What if I have a piece of bread I want to give you? How am I supposed to do that if I can't even call you over by name? Come on already, tell me your name. What're you, mute or something?"

At last the man spoke: "Please call me whatever you like."

"Figures, soon as I mention food, you speak up. Sorry, but I don't have any bread. I see you're not from here. Your accent gives you away. Now I understand why you weren't talking. A lot of people hate foreigners for no reason. Rumor has it the virus was brought here by foreigners. Anything bad always gets blamed on others. You sick?"

He shook his head.

"Of course you are. Who wouldn't be after floating down the sewer like that? Diarrhea is a sickness too, and I've seen with my own eyes that you've had the runs since you got here. Not that I care. You can't help but get sick down here. But anyway, what would you like me to call you? I can never remember foreign names, so it'd be better if you pick something common. Those are easy to remember."

He considered telling the old man his real name, which had long since lost all meaning, but he abandoned the idea. It would be too difficult for the old man to pronounce anyway.

"Hey, how about the name Mol?" the old man asked. "It's stitched on your shirt. Well, okay, I'm wearing it now, so you could also call me Mol, if you like. I change my name all the time. Do you like that name? I like it. Common names are useful."

The man nodded. As a matter of fact, he did like the name. Mol was the name he had to find, and it was the only name he knew in that country.

The old man gave him a name and tolerated his presence because he mistook himself as having something worth taking. He seemed to think the man would help if looters came along. Whenever he heard footsteps, the old man would look around wildly until the steps had faded, and when he slept, he used the knapsack that held all of his belongings as a pillow. While up on the surface, he never set his bag down for even a second. And yet for all of that fear, the old man's knapsack held nothing more than a picnic mat, a blanket that reeked of piss, a filthy toothbrush that looked like it had been used to polish boots, and a dented camping pot that he used as a bowl.

The old man gingerly pushed himself up, tiptoed to the end of the sheet of plywood he had placed on the ground to mitigate the chill, and urinated into the water. Then he sat back down again, took some food that had clearly come from the garbage out of a plastic bag he kept stashed at his side, and in defiance of his own sluggish movements just a moment before, began to wolf it down. The food was gone in a flash, but the man had grown used to seeing people eat this way. Naturally the old man shared none of it with him. It would have been no different if they were good friends who shared heart-to-heart conversations. Likewise, he had no intention of begging for food from the old man. What the old man had really meant was that if the other man came across any-thing to eat, he had to be the one to share it. But when it came to scavenging through trash, age or fitness made no difference: the old man's chances of procuring food were much higher.

Besides, watching the way the old man ate made it difficult to even breathe the same air. The old man ate all of his
food from the camping pot, which he kept with him always,
then dipped the pot in the sewer to clean it. The sewer with
its tarry black, nauseatingly foul-smelling water. The water
was so acidic that not even bacteria could live in it.

One day, in the middle of eating, the old man let out a
stifled scream and hurled the pot at him. He knew the old
man wasn't aiming at him on purpose. He was cold but not
ill-tempered. The pot bounced off of the man's chest and
fell to the ground. A chunk of cold rice rolled out. The
fallen food glimmered whitely against the dirty ground.
The man felt drawn to that strange white light and was
debating whether to pick it up and eat it—after all, the old
man had basically thrown it away, and he was the one
who got hit by it—but before he could decide, the over-
turned pot rattled and started to move. Something wriggled
out from under it. A rat. He quickly grabbed the pot and
brought the back of it down on the rat before it could scramble away. The rat tried again to escape. He tightened his
grip and pressed down hard. He was damned if he was
going to lose his food to a rat. The sensation of something
bursting traveled up through his arm. The ground he stood
on felt suddenly hollow. All at once he remembered the decision he had once made never to kill another rat. Back then,
he had told himself that he would sooner be a rat than kill
another.

"You're fast, kid," the old man said, sounding genuinely impressed, as he snatched up the food he had thrown.

It was unexpected, coming from someone who had surely resorted to eating things worse than rats to survive. But the man soon learned that, despite their tolerance of dirt, none of the sewer people, including the old man, could tolerate rats. No one yet knew the source of the virus, and rumors were rife that rats were carriers.

He picked up the camping pot smeared with the rat's burst entrails, blood, and brain matter, and tossed it over to the old man, who dipped it in the tarry black sewer water as usual to clean it. He didn't put his hand in the water but simply held the pot against the current (though it was dubious whether that water was actually moving) until it had cleaned itself. It took several tries of dipping the pot and holding it up to check whether the smears of blood and chunks of intestines and gray fur had washed off, but once it was clean, the old man gave it a quick wipe against the shirt he was wearing and refilled it with food.

After that, the man passed the time by killing rats—first, at the old man's request whenever one came sniffing around, and later voluntarily, whenever one caught his eye. It was boring to have to sit or lie around all the time waiting for his leg to heal. Since he had to eat, he took brief trips up to the surface during the day to rummage through the trash, but his leg dragged and made it difficult to find enough to sustain himself. He gradually spent less and less time aboveground. He ate as little as possible and urinated into the sewer like the other men. At that rate, it would not be long before he willingly participated in that which he had not yet once brought himself to do, in that which was the absolute inverse of all of his long-cherished beliefs regarding personal hygiene and the maintaining of cleanliness, which he believed were absolutely mandatory if you were to call yourself a human being, in other words, in the laying bare of his most private acts of excretion.

Being prone to frequent earthquakes, Country C distributed information to its citizens on what to do in the event of one via television and printed notices. These information alerts listed camping toilets as one of the very first things that had to be secured following a major earthquake. While it would only take a couple of days to get food and water to people, even with the roads damaged and unusable, the task of finding a place to relieve their other physiological needs fell to each individual. For those who did not own camping toilets, they were advised to use manholes instead. That is, they were asked to urinate and defecate into the city's manholes, right into the place where the man now resided.

While sitting still, waiting for a rat to appear, staring down a dark and narrow passage where a rat was sure to come along eventually, he felt that he himself was one big, oversized, useless rat. And yet his reason for crouching there, ready to pounce, was that only when he caught a rat did he feel he was not totally worthless, not trash, not a rodent of a man.

The first step to killing rats was to figure out where they traveled. That was easier than he thought. Rats stuck to the same paths, so you only had to watch and wait. Once a rat's path to its scavenging ground was set, it did not vary or swerve from that course. When you saw a rat more than once on the same path, it was likely that it was the same rat. As a rule, they did not stray farther than twenty yards from their nests.

Sometimes he caught a rat, but usually he failed. Rats came and went whenever they pleased, with no regard for the man crouching as still as a stone near the places they were sure to appear. When he did manage to kill one of the rats glancing around warily at its surroundings, he was filled with an unfamiliar surge of pleasure. He would stare long and hard at the bright red innards bursting out of the filthy gray hide, like an overripe pomegranate split and spread open to the sun, and then watch as others walked past, treading on the little corpse until it was just a smeared clot of blood and fur.

The rats meant he no longer got caught up in the petty arguments that broke out all the time in the sewer. No one picked a fight with him as he hunched in corners all day waiting for rodents to appear. They seemed to think that rats weren't the only thing he was capable of killing, having witnessed him grabbing whatever was at hand and smashing it down on top of a rat, or catching and killing one with his bare hands when nothing else was available. But he didn't care what they thought. He was happy to be free of other people's pointless meddling.

He left the dead rats aboveground in a pile at the base of one of the bridges. There was nowhere else to discard them. They were dead anyway, and it didn't matter what he did with them. He could have left them right where he killed them. But what he wanted was to get them as far away from himself as possible. The things he had to discard were not dead, dried-up flowers, or scraps of paper covered in cute doodles, or tissues used to blow his nose, they were rats with dangling entrails.

On occasion, he left the dead rats down in the sewer instead of taking them aboveground. The others didn't seem to care. They might pull a face when they noticed, but that was all. Human bodies floated past sometimes (even the old man had mistaken him for a corpse when he fished him out), and they would pull them in, look for anything they could take, and strip them of their clothes. They all knew that the dead were merely dirty, unsanitary breeding grounds for bacteria; what caused real harm were the living. And so they were lenient when it came to leaving dead things lying around. Regardless of what it was, even a disemboweled rat, the dead caused no harm.

Everything was the same as before. The streets were still filled with trash. Burst garbage bags with their contents exposed left dirty smears and smells on the asphalt. The roads were tangled and noisy with cars, and few pedestrians were in sight.

And yet something felt off. He soon discovered the source. As he stood lost in thought in the middle of the trash-strewn pavement, he was nudged out of the way by the sound of a garbage truck blaring its horn at him. Two men in protective suits jumped down and tossed the long-neglected garbage into the truck's gaping mouth. He wondered if this meant the garbage collectors had won their strike. Dozens of trucks were taking the trash away to be burned or buried. The roar and clatter of the giant vehicles was the sound of torn seams being sutured, of gaping cracks being filled.

Some shops were still shuttered, of course, but most were open for business. And though there weren't many shoppers, aside from the peculiarities of piled-up trash, pedestrians in hazmat suits, and black swarms of flies, he could have been standing on any other lively shopping street in any other city. Unchanging displays of products for sale filled the windows, and shop owners leisurely glanced out at the street until the occasional customer came by and could be ceremoniously ushered in.

The man figured the lack of people out and about was because they were all at work or school, in the places where daily life was maintained. He realized this after seeing a swarm of men in suits pour out the front entrance of a building just as he passed by. The men tiptoed carefully around the trash in the street as they went into nearby restaurants or looked at their watches and rushed off to appointments. It was noon, lunchtime for office workers. They had reported to work in the morning, socialized with their coworkers, taken care of the morning's business, chatted about what they wanted for lunch, and then left the building to eat, just as they did every day. Judging from the blithe way they carried themselves, he could tell that they had done this not only that very day but also the day before, and the day before that, and the days that he had spent killing rats in the tunnels below the city while waiting for his leg to heal, the day he was thrown into the sewer by vagrants, the day he leapt into garbage, and all of the days he'd spent quarantined in his apartment while the virus killed people and the number of the infected exploded.

Despite the high rate of infection, the increasingly high death rate, and the continuing lack of a vaccine, everyday life itself remained immune. People kept reporting to work and going to school and selling products. They may have been living in an age of contagion, but there were still clients to be met to ensure the continuation of business. There were things to learn and schools to get accepted to, and other schools and after-school classes that had to be attended in order for that to happen. There were products that had to be exported, and imports that had to be sold at a reasonable markup. As the infected increased exponentially, some schools were closed, but the students, who had not a second of study time to waste, crowded into private after-school classes, causing the number of infected to increase all the more. Thousands of parents descended upon college fairs, and so many young job seekers showed up at a job fair held by a major corporation, against the advice of the authorities, that they ran out of applications. Some places of business experienced mass contagion and were ordered to shut down, but since following government orders would put them at risk of bankruptcy, they fired the sick employees instead and disinfected the office equipment with powerful chemicals.

Chances of infection were high, and the ranks of the dead continued to swell, but no one knew whether they would fall ill or not, nor whether if they did fall ill they would die or not. While the truth of the virus remained clouded, everyday life revealed its own true form: in fissures that opened and cracks that widened the moment it was neglected. Everyday life was like a newborn baby still too weak to lift its own head. It may look peaceful, sleeping there on its stomach, but the threat of sudden, unexpected death looms. You leave the baby resting there, and the next thing you know its neck has snapped, or it has rolled off the bed and injured itself, or buried its face in the blanket and suffocated. And yet you cannot watch over it every second.

Of course, the epidemic did bring changes to some of the more minute corners of daily life. People went to great lengths to avoid setting any dates or appointments, and when they were unavoidably forced to meet, they did not shake hands or exchange business cards. Meetings were conducted from behind surgical masks, and condolences were offered along with their first how-do-you-dos. All was forgivable. They did not touch other people's belongings, and when obliged to use public facilities, they wore disposable plastic gloves. They refrained from using public transportation, as they dared not touch the handles and straps in the buses and subway trains, which might have been touched by the infected. Stair railings and elevator buttons were avoided. People kept their dust masks on, and when they went to a place where many people would be gathered, they took out their hazmat suits and put them on, just as they would a business suit. They avoided the trash-strewn streets and did not disturb the trash piled in front of their homes. The biggest impact the epidemic had on people was not infection and death but rather suspicion of others for fear of exactly that. Every person except for themselves was a potential pathogen, and every place outside of their own homes was dirty beyond belief and had viruses floating in the air.

Official announcements that the epidemic had become a pandemic were posted all over the city. Public loudspeakers blared out entreaties at regular intervals like the chimes of a clock, urging citizens not to take any chances with their personal hygiene as the authorities were likewise beefing up preventative measures to fight the disease.

Health centers in every district were expanded, and quarantine levels rose. In addition to the fumigants used by the sprayer trucks, aerial sprayings and disinfection services for private residences would soon begin. According to rumors coming out of districts that had already reinforced their disease control measures, workers were dragging manual sprayer pumps inside buildings to disinfect them—residents complained that the spray reeked of mothballs and sulfur. Many gagged at the smell and their skin broke out in rashes, but they stifled their nausea and refrained from treating their rashes with ointments. Because rashes were among the symptoms of infection, they feared they would be mistaken for being ill if they were seen purchasing medicine.

Stories continued to abound regarding the epidemic, but none of it amounted to anything more than hearsay. No one knew the truth. The more exaggerated the information, the further the rumors spread. But the one comfort was the fact that, still, far more deaths were caused by traffic accidents, chronic disease, and old age than by the virus making its rounds.

The security guards stood stock-still, in the at-ease position, with their hands behind their backs. But they looked less like they were ready to pull their weapons the instant danger presented itself than like they were enjoying watching the occasional passerby outside the front door.

The man stared hard at one of the guards. The full hazmat suit and dust mask left only a small part of the body exposed—eyes, forehead—making it difficult to tell whether it was the same guard he had spoken to last time. When the guard approached him, clearly intent on kicking out this shabby-looking interloper, he explained that he wanted to check the status of his request. Though he had practiced the question several times on his way there, he still stumbled over the words. This was enough to make the guard realize that he was a foreigner and decide to hear the man out rather than kick him out. The guard asked if he needed help. When the man repeated his question about the request form that he had submitted, the guard strolled over to the counter and opened the same drawer as before. It was stuffed with request forms, just as before. The guard slowly flipped through the sheets of paper, one by one, checking to see if the man's form was among them. But the guard's leisurely movements were not some earnest response to the man's inquiry; rather, they were his way of showing off the one privilege he could call his own.

"Your application isn't here," the guard said, closing the drawer. "But that could mean anything. It could mean good news, or it could mean bad news. Do you understand?"

The man nodded and asked, "So if it's good news, then I've been granted a meeting?"

"If you were granted a meeting, they would have contacted you by now. Have you heard from anyone? If not, that could mean it's still in process."

"And if it's bad news?"

"Bad news means your application was rejected, or your request was discarded due to some clerical error before it could be reviewed by the higher-ups. It's unfortunate, but that sort of thing does happen all the time."

"Is there any way of finding out?"

"Not as things currently stand. I've got nothing to tell you."

"You're the only one here I can ask."

"Look, I'm just a security guard. I greet visitors, I take request forms, and I send the forms upstairs. The rest of the time, my job is to stand here looking friendly and intimidating at the same time. Oh, and the other important thing I do is if someone drops a tissue, I pick it up, and if the floor gets dirty, I mop it. That's why I'm extra busy on rainy days. I have to spend the whole day mopping the floor. And each time I get an earful about how the lobby is the face of the company. Do you understand?"

"Yes. So, how can I find out whether my request was accepted or not?"

"You have to ask the person in charge upstairs. To meet that person, you can fill out this form—"

"My request is very urgent."

"Yeah, I'm sure it is. All requests are urgent. But look. Even before this mayhem started, we had thousands of employees working here. Sure, some of the sick ones got weeded out, but most are still here, plugging away at their jobs. Everyone has a job to do, no matter what's going around. In fact, most of the employees don't bother to leave the building. When you do see someone leaving, it's either because they're suspected of being sick and are getting kicked out, or they took it upon themselves to take a break. This entire building is basically one big clean room. Every single person who comes here to sell something or meet with an employee—yourself included—has to fill out a meeting request form. No exceptions. We get hundreds of these forms a day. In fact, we get so many that we had to hire someone just to go through them. One guy came in here looking for an employee whose parent had died—he had to fill out a form, too. Like I said, no exceptions. That may sound cruel, but rules are rules. Can't do anything about it. I was the one who told him to fill out a form, and of course I was the one who took shit for it. It's not even up to me to decide whose form is accepted! The applications were so backed up that by the time his request for a meeting was accepted, the funeral had already happened. Another time, one of the employees' sons was in a car accident and they needed blood from him for a transfusion. I wasn't the one on duty that time, but it made no difference. None of us security guards have the authority to okay an application. Same situation then, too. By the time his request went through, it was too late. Couldn't even give blood to his own son. From what I heard, they shared a rare blood type. Who knows? Maybe the story was exaggerated . . . but I guess your situation is just as urgent? Please, by all means, let me help you. How about if I move your application to the top of these hundreds of other applications? That's the only thing I can do. I have no idea how they handle these upstairs. Oh, wait. I keep forgetting you're not from here. Do you understand?"

The security guard stared at him and smiled. The man was anxious and wanted to ask more questions, such as how long he would have to wait to find out the results of his application, and whether he would need to fill out another application if his request was rejected. But when faced with the guard's friendliness that came purely from lack of interest and his show of understanding for a matter that did not pertain to him, the man realized there was no point in asking anything at all. And yet, he found it difficult to walk out of there. After a while, another man, relatively well-dressed, came in and complained to the security guard that the application he had filed several days earlier still had not been received upstairs. When he heard the guard give the other man the exact same explanation, he finally left.

It would take a very long time for his application to get processed, and even then he might not be able to meet with Mol. He could stand in front of the building all day and wait for Mol to come by, but that was just as pointless. He had talked to Mol over the phone only twice, and no more. His grasp of the language was not enough to have what you would call a proper conversation. Even if he stood there holding up a cardboard sign, he would still only find Mol if Mol walked up to him first, and there was little chance of that happening. Mol could walk right past him without him recognizing Mol. In fact, the security guard he'd just spoken to could have been Mol himself, and he still would have been none the wiser.

"There's got to be a way," the old man said.

"It's impossible without identification."

The old man had trouble understanding the man's accent. He repeated himself several times, but the old man continued on without any indication of whether he had understood.

"I'm sympathetic but not lenient. I don't mind helping people who are down on their luck, but I can't stand stupid people. I hate stupid people the most. When they're too stupid to grasp what's going on, I try to tell myself it's because they're too nice or maybe just too naïve. They're the ones who mess things up in the end. But don't tell me you're hoping to fly back first-class or something?"

"You mean there might be a way?"

"Yeah, but you'll never find it on your own. You don't know anyone, and you'll just hurt your leg again if you start running around. Your leg may have healed, but it looks terrible, which means you won't have an easy time of getting the other thing you need."

The old man grinned, exposing his yellow teeth. His breath was foul.

"What's the other thing?"

"Money!"

His face dropped, and the old man hurried to add, "Don't forget. The less likely you are to have money, the more you need it. In other words, it's time for you to figure out where to get some."

He stared at the old man and waited for him to continue. The old man let him stew for a moment and then reluctantly asked, "Have you been to the harbor? Ever been on a boat?"

He nodded.

"Well, these are different kinds of boats than the ones you've been on. I'm talking about container ships. You just have to, you know, export yourself. Back to your home country. That's where you're trying to get to, right? Box yourself up like merchandise."

"Export myself?"

"Yeah, export. Don't worry, *no one* would want to buy you. Who on earth would buy a dirty thing like you, unless it's to use you as a slave? I just mean pack yourself inside a box. A big, wooden crate. Of course, you can't just get in the box and go. You need supplies. And that's where money comes in, you see? Before you get in the crate, you need, you know, some kind of breathing apparatus or whatnot. My point is, money will get you that stuff. You'll need it to breathe and stay alive. So you've got to scrape some cash together. Smugglers don't make all that money for nothing. Then, let's see . . . after you have your supplies, you plaster those invoices, the kind with barcodes, onto yourself. You'll need that to make it through inspection. Then your crate is loaded onto the ship. After a while, thousands of other wooden crates are loaded onto the ship with you, and you're off. Rolling back and forth with the waves until you're home free!"

As a matter of fact, the man had heard of people leaving the country that way before, but as with all rumors, the old man's knowledge was only hearsay. As he listened to the old man talk, he wondered how he might be able to earn some money, and the thought made him impatient. To his surprise, his impatience pleased him. Impatience and fear both spring from anticipation of the future. And if you're not anticipating anything, then there's no reason to rush.

The old man said to come talk to him again after he'd found some money and lay down with his back turned. Just then, the man heard the dull metal clunk of the manhole cover opening. The cover had to be opened with a key, so none of the sewer dwellers ever used it. A breeze blew in, and a rag or a towel that someone had left hanging on the ladder flapped as if in greeting.

The first thing to appear was the round beam of a flashlight. The beam landed on the dark floor at the base of the ladder. The man wondered who would appear in its spotlight. Two legs clad in a thick hazmat suit poked in. They stepped on the cloth hanging from the rungs as they made their way down. He heard the owner of the cloth start to curse and then instantly turn quiet upon realizing that the shoes that had trampled on his cloth were heavy army boots.

As the rest of the hazmat suit came into view, the flashlight swung more ruthlessly across their faces. Several of the vagrants who had lain there unmoving, lazy and indifferent, like stains permanently etched into the ground, slowly sat upright as the beam landed on them. They began to whisper among themselves. It was the first time anyone dressed in a hazmat suit had appeared inside the sewer.

At last, the man wielding the flashlight was fully visible. A dead rat dangled from an oversized silver glove. He held it by the tail; each time he moved, the rat's body dangled and swayed. He spun it around in circles like he was getting ready to toss it and then chucked it hard at one of the vagrants lying nearby. No one screamed. There was no point. A dead rat couldn't steal your food. The vagrant nonchalantly picked the rat up by its tail and flung it back at the man with the flashlight. The flashlight man flinched and jumped out of the way.

Then, as if to save face, the flashlight man took an intimidating stance and asked the vagrant a question. They were too far away for the man to hear what was being asked, but he thought he made out the word "rat." He tried to think of what sorts of questions one would ask about rats. The first that came to mind was, "Why did you kill this rat?" But why would anyone bother to ask that? Rats were the kind of animal that pretty much anyone would regard as needing to be killed. Next, he thought, "Why did you leave this dead rat under the bridge?" and "Why didn't you kill *more* rats?" and "Why did you kill it so viciously?" He also considered: "Who killed this rat?" and "What did you use to kill it?" But he couldn't imagine why anyone would want to know those things either.

From the whispered responses to the flashlight man's question, he gathered that they were blaming someone for the rat. He wondered what was happening, but before he could be certain of anything, the old man, who was sitting near the flashlight man, swiveled his head around and pointed directly at him.

The flashlight shone on him. He squinted in the glare and thought maybe the question hadn't had anything to do with rats after all. Maybe "rat" was just figurative. Back in his home country, there were plenty of idiomatic expressions involving rats, and it was no doubt the same in this country. The question he feared most was, "Where is that little rat-fuck?" If that's what was asked, then that meant the flashlight man was a detective. But even if the two countries had an extradition treaty, no one would bother coming all the way down into the sewers just to track down another country's criminal.

That thought alone made him unsure of whether to run or not, and while he hesitated, the flashlight man came closer. He took a few slow steps back and then turned and ran beneath the tangle of pipes, past the vagrants sitting and lying on the ground. The beam of light stayed right on his tail. He was soon out of breath and had just thought to himself that if he was going to dive into the water then now was the time, when he stumbled. It wasn't from exhaustion. Someone had stuck out a leg to trip him.

The light illuminated his face. The flashlight man and several others who had come down the ladder with him grabbed hold of the man. They took his temperature and pried open his jaw to shine the light down his throat. He struggled and tried to twist his body out of their clutches so he could escape, and kicked at the man to his right. The man to his right struck him on the legs as hard as he could with a nightstick.

"Stop fighting!" the man to his right said. "You'll thank me later. You'll thank me for not letting you get away."

He cursed at the man to his right in his native tongue, knowing that no one there would understand him. The man to his right barked with laughter.

"Remember this moment. This is how it goes for us. We bust our balls to get work done, and not a word of thanks to show for it. Instead, we get kicked and cussed at."

The man was dragged aboveground, with the old man trailing behind as if to see him off. Outside, the flashlight man handed the old man a few coins. When he saw the old man smile and take the money, his yellow teeth bared, the man's head ached as if a monkey were clinging to it.

THREE

The routine was simple and straightforward. He got out of bed at the sound of the bell: a short, repetitive, mechanical-sounding melody that echoed through the barracks. After a quick washing up, he and the other men stood in rows and had their temperatures checked. If their temperature was high or they had a cough, they were sent to a separate examination room, and if they were within normal range, they were sent to the mess hall for breakfast. Some took pains to raise their temperature on purpose, so they could take a break from working while getting a secondary inspection in the exam room. They would rub their hands together hard and then place their heated palms against their foreheads, or purposefully wait at the end of the line, jogging and running in place or holding their breath until they got to the front, in order to make themselves flushed and warm. If the secondary health inspection revealed more symptoms, they were sent to a nearby hospital. And if the complete checkup they received there revealed multiple matching symptoms, or so the man was told, then they were removed from the quarantine barracks and sent to an isolation ward on the outskirts of the city. Nobody wanted to go to the isolation ward. No one had ever returned from there. Though they said the mortality rate was low, nobody was going to give former vagrants unlimited medical care.

After breakfast, they returned to the barracks where they changed into hazmat suits, received their packed lunch rations, and boarded the work vans for their assigned districts. Their lunches usually consisted of steamed white rice squeezed into fist-sized chunks. For someone like him, who had been homeless long enough to lose all pickiness and be left with only appetite, he had no particular complaints about the food, other than the fact that the tiny amount was only enough to take the edge off of his hunger.

The person who had come down into the sewer looking for him was the head of a door-to-door extermination team. Pairs of men were dispatched from each team to search individual residences for pests. They were absurdly understaffed. Since it was not clear how exactly the epidemic had been spreading, people were resorting to superstition and knowledge of past outbreaks. The epidemic this time was suspected of being caused by rats, just like another epidemic that had once terrorized the world. The only proof of this was the plague of rats infesting the city. The rat population had boomed. Rats bit children fast asleep in bed. They defecated inside closets and broke dishes in kitchens. When spotted astride crossbeams or crawling up to kitchen ceilings, eliciting screams, they free-fell from their perches and shot like arrows across the kitchen floor, as if their plan all along had been to startle and alarm. And yet for all of that, the number of rats was not so unusual. They were merely more conspicuous than before, and that was due to the trash in the streets, not to the virus.

Some believed that the supposed increase in the rat population was a sign that an earthquake was coming. A few years earlier, an earthquake had struck ninety miles west of the center of Country C. It was a memorably powerful quake that left six thousand dead. And before that earthquake as well, countless numbers of rats had appeared, infesting the city.

Rumors of an impending major quake had long been going around among the city residents. A hypothesis presented thirty years earlier by a professor of seismology at one of the universities was being exaggerated and circulated out of context. The professor had extracted statistics from relatively old magnitude-five earthquakes and suggested that they repeated themselves at regular intervals. Several researchers had pointed out that the figures the professor used were statistically meaningless, but his work had caused a sensation back then, and now that much time had passed, it had resurfaced.

It was the official opinion of the authorities that the rats had nothing to do with earthquakes or the current epidemic.

But mere opinions were powerless to stop the fear of a major quake, proliferation of rumors, or spread of disease. Fear and rumors and viruses shared a similar nature. They bore a tremendous vitality of their own, oblivious to human efforts to stamp them out. They could spread rapidly even while offering no clue to their routes of transmission. And they would burn for a long, long time, like dry grassland, only to vanish in an instant as if doused with water.

Thus, the drafting of the temporary exterminators. Rather than fussing over how to control an invisible virus, killing the vermin that infested each home was good optics and effective at putting rumors to sleep. Hunting down the vermin hidden inside people's homes was enough to convince citizens that no wonder they were all getting sick—just look at all those rats they were cohabiting with.

The exterminators were supposed to be drafted from among volunteers, but hardly anyone stepped up. Not only did they know the work would put them at risk of infection, it was only a temporary position and the pay was low. Being temporary workers meant they received no protection under labor laws, were exempt from unemployment and job search benefits, and were not even eligible for minimum wage. So the authorities had no choice but to forcibly draft workers from the nonprofessional population—most of whom were vagrants—and put together teams. That was why his own boss had braved the manhole after seeing all of those limp rat corpses piled up under the bridge like spoils of war.

But regardless of whether the authorities were wrong about the rats or not, his being captured by the extermination team was, just as the man who'd hit him with the nightstick said, a stroke of luck. To say that he had been captured made it sound unjust. In truth, he was grateful to the men. Grateful to them for pulling him from that dirty sewer, for giving him clean food at set times, for stopping him before he jumped into that black sewage, and most of all, for giving him a shiny silver hazmat suit.

Whenever he wore that giant suit that covered him from head to toe, he felt sluggish and heavy. Like an overfed baby. The suit was so heavy that after a full day of wearing it, his shoulders ached and he was drenched in sweat. For someone like him, forced to spend long hours stalking rats in a crouched and huddled position, the puffy, oversized suit was cumbersome and kept getting in the way. But when he returned to the dorm at the end of the workday and had to remove the suit, he felt like he was facing down pathogens barehanded. Even when he slept, he rested his head on his folded-up suit instead of a pillow. He had not always done that. But fights were constantly breaking out in the barracks. The exterminators bickered over the smallest things, bickering soon turned to punching, and when that happened, hazmat suits would get ripped, just to cause each other grief. The owner of the ripped suit would despair, as if infection were imminent and they would fall ill at any second, and the person who had ripped the suit would apologize, as if they had just delivered the fatal virus themselves, and hand over their own suit. Whenever he saw those men apologize for losing their temper and blame it on the rat poison being too toxic, he clutched his suit tightly to him like a lover.

As demand increased, the suits were replaced with bulk shipments of low-quality sauna suits that had no protective features at all. Some of the randomly issued suits were so poorly sewn that shoddy cotton batting stuck out where the stitches had given way. They were closer to snowsuits stuffed with fiberfill than proper hazmat suits. The cheap suits were clearly intended for the temporary workers. Nevertheless, the man cherished his suit. It signified more than just safety to him. Though there were people on the streets without them now, most were still clad in protective gear. Wearing it signified that you were the same as everyone else. And being the same as everyone else meant not having to think about your own existence. It meant that, other than becoming infected and having your everyday life ruined, you had nothing to fear.

The sky was pitch black. Wind whispered through the trees. From somewhere came the barely audible snap of a twig. He crouched on all fours. The ground was blanketed with old pine needles that absorbed the sound of his footfalls. There were no passersby and no one entering the building, so no one saw him hiding there in the darkness. He heard a crunch and the sound of grass stirring. It was a rat. A rat with shiny black, beady eyes stopped at the boundary stone marking the edge of the garden and stared directly at him. If it came any closer, he would be inclined to kill it, but he was afraid the noise would alert the security guards to his presence. The rat likewise seemed afraid that the man might come closer. It quickly turned and disappeared back the way it had come, along the path it knew best. Concerned that another rat might appear, the man hurried to his feet.

No matter how many times he had stalked out the building, the lobby never emptied for even a second. Three guards were always on duty, employees came and went in large groups, visitors filled out forms at the counter to the right of the entrance. At eight in the evening, the three security guards were relieved by the night shift. There would still be a few employees passing through the lobby, dressed in their own protective suits and dust masks. At ten, two of the guards paired up to patrol the outside of the building. They strolled once around the perimeter to check that nothing was amiss with the security system, a process that took only about twenty minutes, during which the remaining guard stood blank-eyed next to the bust of the founder in the lobby. When the patrol ended, the metal security shutters were rolled down over the front entrance, the lobby lights were dimmed, and one of the three guards went off duty. Few employees came through the lobby after that. The building was only accessible after-hours through the back entrance, which had the same type of automatic sliding door as the front entrance. At eleven, one of the two guards standing watch at the back entrance would also go off duty and retire to the guardroom out back. The final guard stayed behind in the well-lit lobby. He would pace constantly, never dozing, keeping a watchful eye on his surroundings until exactly midnight when he locked the back entrance, checked that the building alarm, which was outsourced to another company, was turned on and functioning, and turned off all the lights. The only time the lobby was left unguarded was if the one guard alone on duty from eleven to midnight, or earlier, when the other two were patrolling the perimeter, could not withstand the call of nature and had to go to the toilet. But the man had yet to see that happen.

It had cost the man all of the money he'd saved to bribe his boss into letting him skip the night shift. The amount must have been more than what he thought, because after he struggled to get the words out, his boss had happily loaned him a business suit as well.

"I take it you're seeing someone? And every night, from the looks of it."

The man smiled and did not answer.

"You're going to wear yourself out," his boss said. "Catching rats by day and women by night. Quite the busy man, you are."

The boss's suit was a little big on him. It looked like the kind of thing a cheap man would buy his growing son.

Just as he was starting to think that he may as well head back early this time instead of waiting until midnight, the security guard slowly stretched his stiff muscles and gazed up at a large clock on the wall. There were only twenty minutes left in his shift. The guard seemed to be debating something. He glanced up at the clock again and stood. He looked like he was considering whether to go to the toilet, but instead he raised his arms overhead, stretched his body out long and tall, and sat back down.

The man's shoulders sagged as he realized he had spent another evening hiding in vain. His bladder was full to bursting. In the past, he would have unzipped right there and taken care of business. But instead, he tentatively made his way to the back door. When he stepped into view, the guard snapped to attention as if greeting a high-ranking manager.

"I'm sorry to bother you, but could I use the facilities?" the man asked.

The guard's stiff expression relaxed as he studied the man in the business suit. Other than the fact that it was a little big on him, the suit was more or less impeccable. The man stood stock-still for fear of straining his already taut bladder.

"Must be pretty urgent," the guard said. "Even your face has gone yellow."

The guard pressed the button to activate the sliding glass door and gestured politely toward the restrooms next to the emergency stairwell.

The man took his time relieving himself and washing his hands. When he came out, the guard was sitting as stiffly as ever, his back turned to him. The man cracked open the door to the stairwell, half-expecting an alarm to start blaring. But his trespass was silent, muting all worry that he had tripped an alarm. Only his footsteps echoed in the darkened stairwell.

The door to the nineteenth floor, Mol's department, was locked tight. A warning sign in red letters written on white paper was taped to the metal door: AREA UNDER QUARANTINE; ENTRANCE STRICTLY PROHIBITED. The man went up to the twentieth floor instead. The door was open. The walls and floor of the hallway were a uniform murky green. The ceiling was a brighter shade of green, but the bright fluorescents made it look like everything had been painted white. The parallel rows of long fluorescent bulbs lit everything so brightly that the air itself looked cold. Square doors stood at regular intervals down the length of the hallway, all shut tight. None of the rooms could be entered without a keycard.

He stood there quietly. Just then, a male employee appeared abruptly, as if he had tunneled straight through a wall. The employee carried a towel in one hand and seemed to be headed for the restroom. The man slowly approached the employee and asked where he could find Mol's department.

"Some of the people from that department used to work on this floor," the employee said.

"That's good to know. I'm looking for someone who works there."

"Well, it is and isn't good. I heard most of the people in that department were fired. They either got sick or are being monitored for signs of infection. It won't be easy to find the person you're looking for. On the other hand, if you had found them sooner, you'd be infected too. So that's good news for you."

"Oh, no. That would be terrible if my friend is infected."

"This person is a friend?"

"Yes, but I haven't heard from him in a long time. I felt bad about not calling him even though we work in the same building. I figured since I was here tonight working over-time, I may as well try to find him."

"Is your friend also a foreigner?"

"No. His name is Mol. He's been very kind to me, even though I'm not from here."

"I know the people in that department. But I don't know of anyone there named Mol. I mean, I've heard the name before, so maybe I do know him. You must have been doing a lot of overtime lately. You look tired."

"That's how it is."

"Same for me. I haven't been out of this building in over a month. I guess it's true that when you do nothing but work, work, work, you can't help but suddenly think of old friends. Follow me."

The employee led the way. Just as he had said, it was the kind of night when you couldn't help thinking of old friends. One of those nights where you want to see everyone but can't see anyone.

The office the employee led him to was the same as any other office in any other building. The only difference was that, in a normal office, only one or two employees would be working that late after hours in their scramble to beat out others for prized promotions. The employee told him to wait at the door while he got someone.

A few people glanced over at him as he stood there, but other than that no one paid him any mind. He looked at the hunched backs of the employees as they stared at their computer monitors. Their indifferently turned backs and well-oiled movements told him that he was no threat to them.

After he had stood there for some time, picturing himself being dragged away by a security guard, a man in an industrial-strength dust mask appeared from where the other employee had gone. His button-down shirt was wrinkled, and the sleeves were pushed up to his elbows; he looked like he'd taken a break from working to catch a quick nap. The masked employee directed him into a small conference room that looked like it was intended for visitors there on business. The friendly manner with which the employee treated him, despite the late hour, gave him hope that he would somehow get to meet Mol.

"I understand you're looking for Mol."

"Yes, I'm looking for Mol."

"Are you a foreigner? Your accent . . ."

He nodded.

"I guess I better speak slowly then. Are you aware that Mol is contagious?"

"Excuse me?"

"Ah, you're not. Mol is on sick leave."

"How long has he been sick?"

"I'm not sure. He was among the first to become infected, but I don't remember exactly when that was."

"In that case, maybe I could see the person who took over his duties."

"Took over? If there were such a thing, then we could get sick without any worries. You say you're his friend, but you seem more concerned with his job. We all have so much to do that we're on the verge of dying from overwork. We work and work without a single day off, and yet it just keeps piling up. Every time I look at the endless stack of papers on my desk, all I can do is sigh. Look for yourself: it's almost midnight, but the office is still full. Even in the midst of an epidemic, the one thing that doesn't change is the fact that work has to get done. It's important not to get sick, but I guess what matters more is not letting sickness mess up your work, right?"

The man nodded.

"We're already overloaded, so there's no such thing as 'taking over' other people's work. It wasn't always like that, but as more and more people got sick, it became impossible. At some point, their responsibilities do end up falling to other people, but only when the boss has no choice but to make that order. And no matter how we try to limit outside visitors, people like you just keep showing up. . . . If you get sick, that's it. Game over. The work you did is ruined, lost. Not because you're sick, but because you can't keep working on it. No one can voluntarily take over anyone else's work. The documents the contagious person touched are all scrapped. You can't look at them or touch them anymore. They're useless. Even the person's computer is never turned back on, except in the most extraordinary of circumstances. Sure, you can put on several layers of gloves and try to work the keyboard, but it's too much trouble. Once someone goes on sick leave, their work is either shelved or scrapped."

"What happened with the employee transferred here from the branch office?"

"Branch office? In all my years here, I've never seen anyone from the branch office."

"I'm from the branch office. Mol selected me."

"Oh, so then Mol's not your friend? Sorry, even though we're in the same department, the work we do is completely different. Everyone minds his own business. And in Mol's

case, most of the human resources work he did was conducted under strict confidentiality."

"So you never heard Mol say anything about transferring
an employee from the branch office overseas?"

"It's a big office. Doesn't matter if you're in the same
department. If you don't sit right next to the person or work
on the same projects together, then most of the time you
have no idea what they're up to. Mol and I were close enough
that we'd stop and chat when we saw each other, but that
doesn't mean he would have brought up something like that
with me. The nature of his work meant he never mentioned
specific individuals. That kind of talk tends to spread fast
and never stays secret. If you let a secret get out, it will always
come back to bite you in the end."

"Would it be possible to find out where Mol lives?"

"No, I'm afraid not. Even if I did know, I couldn't tell you.
I've never seen you before in my life. And to be honest, you
keep mispronouncing things, and your grammar . . ."

A troubled look passed over the employee's face, and he
hesitated before continuing.

"He may be a friend of yours, but frankly I doubt whether
you were really transferred here. There was discussion at
some point of transferring a foreign employee to our department. The most fundamental criterion was their ability to
communicate. There was no disagreement whatsoever on
that point. But looking at you now . . ."

The employee ran a careful eye over the man.

"I'm sure you have your strengths. Either you're amazing at your job, or you're very trustworthy."

The employee looked at the clock.

"That's all I know. I've nothing more to say. And now you're out of time."

"What?"

The employee shrugged. The man understood. Through the glass door of the conference room, he saw two guards approaching. The employee opened the door and reprimanded the guards.

"We've been over this. How many more times do I have to tell you that this isn't some public toilet that just anyone can use? You can't keep letting everyone in here."

"We're sorry, sir. He said it was urgent."

After the guards apologized, they turned to the man, bowing their heads slightly as if to apologize to him as well, and took him by the arms, one guard on each side of him. He offered up his arms willingly. Now that he knew Mol was not there, he had no further reason to stay.

While waiting for the elevator, he heard the employee call his name.

"You're not infected, are you?" the employee asked. "It was so long ago that I can't be certain, but I recall hearing that an infected foreigner vanished from the airport."

"I'm not infected."

"I guess our memories can always be wrong. But do you even know what Mol looks like? I bet you don't, do you?"

The man didn't answer.

"It's going to be pretty hard for you to find him then."

The employee smiled knowingly and turned and walked back into the office.

As the man got onto the elevator with the guards, he remembered that Mol was the only person in the country who knew his name. But that did not necessarily mean this employee was Mol. He did not believe in such coincidences. Maybe the employee had taken over Mol's duties after all, despite claiming otherwise. Nevertheless, he could not shake the thought that maybe he had finally met Mol.

His workday began with greeting the homeowner. Once the exchange of formalities was over and he began looking around the yard, most homeowners wished him luck and left for work. He used this time to pretend to work while keeping a close eye on the homeowner as they rushed out the door. Their short, quick steps around the house, their repeated glances at the clock, the way they looked energetic and tired at the same time—it was all so familiar to him. Back in his home country, he and his coworkers probably looked the same when they were rushing off to work. Seeing those busy homeowners reminded him that everyone was still going to school, going to work, going on dates, going shopping, going to the swimming pool for exercise, and each time that happened, his head emptied out and went blank, as if he were realizing for the first time in his life how peaceful the world was without him in it. A cool breeze had begun to blow after nightfall. He'd only been in Country C just long enough to see the seasons change, and yet the life he had lived before coming to Country C felt as distant as something from a previous existence.

Once the homeowners were out of sight, he busied himself with inspecting every corner of the yards and storage sheds that had become his new workplace. There were many paths a rat might take, but the low trees and shrubs that grew behind the houses were among the more probable locations.

It pleased him to sprinkle rat poison along the paths a rat would likely travel and then wait for a rat to appear while gazing at the shadows cast by the shrubs and the dead, dried-up weeds lying in their shade. If he waited long enough, eventually one would emerge from the shade, then a couple more, and then dozens, all letting their guards down, bursting out of the dark toward the food on the surface, and the moment their bodies met the light, their little skulls would explode and they would die. Of course, the one who made that happen was him.

Since rats were not like trains and did not appear right on schedule, the man had no choice but to stay tense. Sometimes he spent nearly half a day waiting, his eyes glazed over, his raised hand numb, before a rat finally appeared. By then, his body would have turned sluggish, his legs cramped, and his arm stiff. As he inhaled the toxic dust that billowed with each thud of the stick he used to smash the rat, he would realize anew that this desperate fight to the death was all for the sake of stopping one measly rat. It reminded him each time of how a single, filthy, ugly rat had recharted his life's course. This rat, too, might very well force him into some strange, new life. Coming to this country, throwing himself into the garbage, living as a vagrant in a park, drifting down the sewer—as unbelievable as it was, it had all started with a single rat. His killing of a rat was what had made the branch manager consider him in the first place. And here he was again, with no particular feelings or attachment to his current life, waiting for chance to bring him another rat, and putting everything he had into killing it.

He heard footsteps approaching. He knew the moment he heard them that it was the homeowner, but he remained crouched and pretended not to notice. When her footsteps were right on top of him, he swung his wooden stick at the ground even though there was no rat. A cloud of gray dust billowed up. The woman stepped to the side to avoid the dust. With a sheepish look, he fingered the food laced with rat poison that he had placed all along the curbstones bordering the flowerbed.

"I thought you were just sitting around, but I guess you've been working after all," the woman said.

He turned to look at her. She must have just come from work. She was smartly dressed and carrying a nice bag. She had the look of a woman who had never experienced anything fearful in her life. Perhaps, at most, being startled by a rat while out walking at night.

"This is how we work," the man said. "Most of our time is spent waiting for rats to appear. We cannot very well go down the rat holes after them. Once we know how they are getting around, we set traps, sprinkle poison, and wait."

"Must be boring."

"It's like digging up fossils or excavating chunks of rock. We must wait it out the same way."

He felt compelled to offer some sort of justification, as he knew it was easy to misinterpret staring vacantly at the shadow of a bush as loafing, but he wasn't sure if he had explained himself properly. He couldn't think of the words he really wanted to say, so he substituted others in their place, which caused him to stammer, and the more he tried to correct his pronunciation, the worse he stumbled. He used words and expressions that meant something similar to what he hoped to say, but he always ended up sounding stiff and formal. Nevertheless, the woman nodded right away as if she had understood him.

"Well, I don't know if this work is as worthwhile as digging up fossils, but it's certainly timely."

"Excuse me?"

"Rats and epidemics. Before, a job like yours would have seemed quite lowly, but now it's a useful and practical profession. Especially compared to someone like me, who can do nothing but scream and wave her hands around when there's a mouse in the kitchen."

He shrugged and smiled but said nothing in response. Despite what she said, rat-catching had always been a timely profession.

"I take it you're not afraid of rats," she said.

"I am afraid."

"How do you deal with it?"

"I don't. I fear them."

"And yet you're so good at catching them."

"Because I get paid to."

"Yes, I forgot this is not a hobby. But there is one thing that's scarier than rats. Do you know what that is?"

"What?"

"People."

"Why is that?"

"Because they transmit disease."

"Rats transmit far more."

"The virus this time is transmitted by people. I could be carrying it, too."

There was an edge to her voice. He looked at her in surprise.

"You can tell whether someone is sick by looking at their face. Especially the color of their lips. Judging by your lips, I'd say you're either sick or about to become sick."

He unconsciously raised one hand to his mouth and remembered that his face was covered by the protective mask on his suit.

"How can you see my lips?"

"I can't, of course. I was just making that up. It's a superstition anyway. A story that's been going around. But everyone believes it."

"Do you always talk to people this way? Scaring them by telling them they're sick?"

"It's just a joke. We always joke that way at work. On days when we don't feel like working, we say we wish we were sick instead. Because then we could take time off work while being treated for free by the government."

"Surely working is better than being sick."

"I don't always feel that way."

"Aren't you afraid of the virus?"

"Cancer is scarier." She looked at him intently and added, "Besides, this virus that's going around is nothing more than the common cold."

"For just a cold, it has killed a lot of people."

"Everyone thinks that. But the mortality rate isn't out of the ordinary. It's not that serious. Sure, people have died from the virus, but more continue to die from cancer and car accidents. And, of course, most deaths are from old age."

"All the same, those people could have lived longer if they didn't get sick."

"That could be said for all deaths. If you don't get in a car, if you don't cross the street, then you won't get in an accident. What's more is that rats have nothing to do with this epidemic. Killing them won't make any difference."

"Says who?"

"Everyone knows it. No one knows if it's true or not, but they're all thinking it. Don't you know it, too?"

"I'm just here to get rid of the rats."

"I sell life insurance for a living. I scare people into thinking that they could die at any moment from the epidemic, but the truth is that I've yet to meet anyone who's infected. I've never even met someone who's met someone who's infected."

"But couldn't that be because everyone who's met someone who's infected has died or is dying?"

"People die for all sorts of reasons. Disease is just one of many causes. Like cancer or traffic accidents. And murder."

"Murder?"

"There are all sorts of terrible ways to die. Consider the rats. Was there any way of knowing they would end up with their guts splattered everywhere? Well, except of course that you're the one who did it."

The woman laughed as if she had made a joke. He didn't find it amusing, but he laughed with her. It occurred to him that it had been a long time since he had laughed.

After the homeowner went inside, he walked around the backyard, collecting the poisoned rats and killing a few strays. When it was almost time for the work van to pick him up, he slowly cut off the rats' tails. His pay was based on the number he caught. The homeowners were supposed to count the corpses, but few welcomed that task. He tied the severed tails together in bundles of ten. Most homeowners didn't even look at the tails when they paid him. He was, of course, supposed to turn over the cash they gave him to his boss, but he soon learned the trick to making more than he had actually earned. Since the homeowners never took the tails from him, he would add in the tails from his previous day's catch while collecting his pay. And since no one ever wanted to examine them too closely, no one had yet questioned why some of the tails were dried up or no longer wet with blood. That was how he had saved enough to bribe his boss.

That day, he was so distracted thinking of other things that his knife moved much slower than usual and he made a rare mistake. The knife came down while his hand was still in the way, and he nearly chopped his finger off. Luckily the blade just missed. But when the blood oozed from the rat's severed tail, he felt his own finger ache as if the blood were flowing from him. He cupped his uninjured finger and gazed in the direction of the woman's house.

While bundling the tails together, he took the previous day's tails from his pocket and smeared them with blood from the fresh tails. By the time his work was done, his protective suit was spattered with blood as usual.

The homeowner took a long look at what he held out to her without even making a face.

"You won't have to worry about rats for the time being, ma'am," the man said. "But it won't last long. It's impossible to kill all of them with poison, and the surviving rats will quickly multiply."

She nodded absentmindedly and stepped closer to him as if to get a better look at the tails.

"Well, they're not exactly dripping with blood," she said.

"The blood has mostly dried by now."

"May I touch them?"

"Of course, you may, but I wouldn't want to if I were you."

"You're touching them right now."

"Only because I have to."

"It's times like this that I envy rats."

"Excuse me?"

"They die instantly. How often do people get to do that? Even with this virus, they say you're sick for a minimum of several months before you die."

"I heard you die within days."

"We must be talking about different diseases then. But, these tails—something's off."

"What are you talking about?"

"The ends are dry. It looks like the blood was smeared on them from the outside rather than coming from the inside."

The woman stared hard at him. Her expression had lost all kindness.

"I believe you're mistaken, ma'am."

"My eyes don't deceive me. That's why I stalled for time. The blood on these dried faster than on the others."

It did not take a second glance to see that the blood was already flaking off of some of the tails.

"This is not the right way to earn money," she said. "I'll pay you, of course. But I want to be clear on that."

The woman went back into the house and up to the second floor to get cash. The stairs went straight up with no landing and were enclosed by walls on both sides, making the passage look extremely narrow. The top of the stairs was cloaked in shadow. She looked like she was dissolving into the dark. By the time her bare feet poked back through the darkness and began to descend the stairs again, he was feeling low, as if he had just woken from a terrible dream.

"Frankly," she said, "I'd rather live with rats than have to hire someone like you. Now I see why you keep the rats even after you kill them. I wonder if your boss knows about this."

She put the cash in his hand and slammed the front door in his face. He stood there a moment. Though it hadn't lasted long, he had enjoyed talking to her. She was the only woman he'd met since coming to Country C who understood his pronunciation with relative ease—or, at least, who pretended to understand him.

She was also now the only person who posed a threat to him. He marveled over the fact that he still had something that could be taken from him, that there was something he could be threatened with, but he feared it at the same time. He cracked open the woman's front door. There was a little time left before the work van arrived to pick him up. His boss, who doubled as their driver, would lay on the horn several times to hurry him up but would never, ever get out of the car.

The sensation of cold air against his body when he slipped back into the house stayed with him until much later, even when he eventually quit his job. Goosebumps covered his skin inside the protective suit. It was a remarkably unfamiliar sensation. He had been revolted by the stink of sweat coming off of his body while wearing the suit, but he had never before felt cold in it. He paused for a moment to take in this strange new sensation, and then continued inside. The house was so dark and quiet that it felt deserted.

While listening closely for sounds of the woman, he saw her coming through a door on the other side of the dining table and ducked into the dark stairwell on reflex. She had not yet seen him, but it was only a matter of time. He held his breath and regretted not having rung the doorbell instead and sought her permission to enter. But he had no time to correct his mistake. Just then, the woman spotted him hiding in the stairwell and froze as if seeing a ghost. She looked ready to scream and run out of the house. He had indeed trespassed, but it was not his intent to cause a scene. He just wanted to plead with her and explain his situation. As he blocked her from leaving, she let out a terrified scream. The scream did not last long. His strong hand wrapped around her mouth. He stammered out apologies, confessing his wrongdoings and begging her forgiveness. He had to cover her mouth or else she wouldn't be able to hear him over her own screams.

He stopped talking and released her. Scared and breathing hard, she backed away from him. As he started his stream of apologies again, she reached for a pair of scissors sitting on top of a chest of drawers. They looked like the kind of scissors used to cut fabric. She aimed the long blades toward him. She was squeezing the handles so tightly that the tendons stood out in clear relief on her hands. He took a step closer, and she raised the scissors a little higher. Having to bow and scrape in shame because of a few measly rats made him miserable, and he resented her for making him feel that way. He took another step closer, and she swung. The blades grazed the back of his hand, but he felt nothing. It frightened her more than him. He wished she would come at him harder. He wanted her to bite him and punch him and drive the scissors into his stomach. That way, in the future, when he was looking back on this moment and on all of the moments that were about to follow, he might feel a little less distressed about it.

The woman bit her trembling lip. He wavered for the briefest of moments, but as he looked around at the darkened house, he reminded himself that he had never dreamt of a life spent killing rats. Nor had he dreamt of a life spent trembling in fear that a career in rat-catching would be taken from him. He snatched the scissors from her without nicking a single finger and clasped her to him. She struggled to free herself. As he squeezed tighter, he wondered what life he *had* dreamt of for himself. He could not remember a single thing that had happened in the past. It was as if everything in his life had happened an eternity ago, or in a dream, or perhaps he had never dreamt of anything at all. The woman kicked at his legs. She was not doing a very good job of escaping him, but her squirming caused him to drop the scissors. If he kept running down the clock like this, everything would be ruined. The work van would arrive any minute, the horn would sound, his boss would wonder why he was taking so long to leave the woman's house, and if the woman screamed loudly enough to be heard all the way outside, he would be arrested.

For no other reason than that it was difficult to keep his grasp on the struggling woman, with no other intent but to stop her from screaming, he fumbled in his pocket and pulled out the dull knife he had found long ago in the trash. He squeezed the handle tight, worried that his sweaty palms might make him drop it, and felt once again the throbbing sensation that had plagued him long ago. The ache in his hand was like a shadow that followed him always, sometimes stretching out long, sometimes shrinking down small, and right now it covered him from head to toe. From inside that ache, he brought the knife to the woman's throat with a familiar gesture. He meant only to scare her. The knife was so dull that there was hardly any difference between the blade and the spine. Stabbing someone with it wouldn't be easy, and even if he did stab her, the wound would not be fatal. But the woman had no way of knowing that. She let out a scream so filled with terror that it sounded pitiful, even to his ears.

As if in response to her scream, a car horn beeped. It sounded like it was right outside. Or it might have been somewhere off in the distance. It was difficult to tell exactly where the sound came from. The woman saw the worry in his eyes and screamed again. He used the knife then, because it was the only way to shut her up. He had meant only to scare her, but the shadow pressed down heavily on him. He waved his hand around wildly, just to get out from under the weight of that shadow. His hand did not stop moving until a gush of blood hit him in the face. Blood spattered on his hand, which he had clenched so hard it was going numb, and all over his protective suit.

The smell of unfamiliar blood cracked the seal on his memory: he knew at once that this had all happened before. The sensation of squeezing a metallic weapon in his hand and of being splattered with blood was entirely different from that of chopping off rats' tails or mercilessly smashing their bodies to bits. The familiarity of the sensation made him understand at last why he had thrown himself into the garbage to escape all those days ago. His first thought was of feeling an odd sort of relief that was incomprehensible even to him. It seemed he had wasted a great deal of time in Country C in pursuit of that relief. And, he thought of his ex-wife. He thought about her round face and nasal voice and kind eyes and pouty lips. He couldn't stop thinking about her. That soft, round face. That whiny, girlish voice. The innocent yet playful gleam in her eyes. The pouty, amorous lips. He dropped to his knees, and the woman fell with a resounding thump beside him. If she died, it wouldn't be from the knife, it would be from the impact of her head against the hard floor. He hunched over and used the hem of her dress to wipe the blood from his suit. Even if she did die, her body would not be discovered right away. People had mostly stopped visiting each other ever since the epidemic had begun. Employees who didn't show up for work were presumed infected and were automatically placed on sick leave.

The sun was already on the verge of setting, but it was so bright outside that he was momentarily blinded. He walked slowly out into the light. The work van had not yet arrived. A garbage truck pulled up, and two men jumped down and got to work tossing the piles of trash in the street into the back of the truck. He gazed vacantly at the sight of the trash being cleanly swept away.

PART THREE

ONE

The mirror on the metal locker in the changing room reflected his gaunt face back at him. The face in the mirror looked hard. He was dizzy, his head as loose as a compass needle, and it made him nauseous. He let out the cough he had been suppressing. The symptoms had not gone away, but they only came at intervals, like a yawn, and never got any better or worse. Along with the cough, his constant slight fever had persisted for a long time. But for all he knew, his usual body temperature might have simply gone up a degree.

His vertigo was about as pronounced as the shaking during the recent earthquake. It wasn't a very big quake. Certainly not the major quake that had long been forewarned. And there had been no signs just before it struck. His apartment shook a little. The aged building suffered a cracked wall and lost a few weathered wooden boards. But he wrongly assumed that the quake wasn't big enough to kill anyone. Some people did die. The moment the buildings began to sway, they mistook it for the big one and jumped out of their windows in fright, thinking only of getting away from the buildings. Other than those people, there were no fatalities.

Though it was fortunate it was a small quake, he couldn't help feeling cheated and therefore despondent. But he soon took heart. The big one would come eventually. There was no telling when. There was no telling where. That was why everyone feared a major quake. To prepare for this eventuality, he had flocked to the supermarket along with all of his team members and bought a camping toilet that looked like a baby's potty and several varieties of canned goods that he would never have otherwise eaten. The quake that did finally come turned out to be so slight that he didn't need any of his supplies. He kept them all stacked under the table in the middle of his living room, in preparation for the big one that might still come one day.

He had been inside a restaurant pantry during the small quake. It was a large, well-equipped pantry. He had moved aside a box of onions and startled a large rat crouching underneath. It scurried over to the wall. He left it alone to escape wherever it wished. It didn't matter. It would have to come out eventually to eat the poisoned bait he'd placed all around the pantry, and when it did, its body would turn stiff and it would die. When he picked up the next box of onions, he spotted a dozen or more dirty, gray rats running single file along the wall and through a hole that led outdoors. He watched the rats fleeing their home in terror. Something was coming. He did not know what.

The rats vanished from sight, and as he lifted the next box containing potatoes, he felt his body tilt. He thought at first it was from the weight of the box. Either it was too heavy, or maybe he was having another attack of vertigo. But then the box was visibly tilting, and the potatoes that filled the box began dropping to the floor like startled rats. He watched the potatoes roll away and realized that it was not the box but the earth that was tilting, and that he, too, was tilting. He lay down flat to keep from falling over, the floor swaying gently beneath him like the bottom of a boat. It had reminded him of an old man he'd met once long ago. An old man with teeth so brown they verged on black. An old man who had told him that he could board a container ship in exchange for money. He had felt thrilled by the old man's claim to be able to send the man anywhere in the world despite never going anywhere himself. Had he boarded a container ship as the old man told him to, he would have crossed the ocean amid this constant swaying with no clue as to where he was.

"I've got good news."

The boss approached the man just as he was about to change into his gray coveralls. His new boss was short and thin and always dressed in dark gray, and he talked in a high-pitched voice, so everyone called him Cricket. When he found out they were calling him that, all he said was, "Hey, at least I'm

not on the extermination list!" which earned him the enduring respect of his work team.

"You don't look so good. Another headache?" His boss
looked worried.

"It's nothing. Happens all the time."

"Shame you can't just chop your head off!" His boss
laughed. "I know an amazing trick for getting rid of head-
aches. Want to know what it is? If you want to stop feeling
your headache, just get a stomachache, a backache, or a
toothache instead!" He laughed again. "I'm just kidding with
you. But it's true that the only way to control an illness is
with an illness."

When the man did not laugh, his boss straightened his
face and lowered his voice.

"This is strictly between you and me, but there's going to
be a review of the temporary employees. I might even be on
the review panel. How about that? What do you think?
Good news, right?"

He wondered if his boss was telling him this as a way of
asking for a bribe, and the more he thought about it, the more
confused he felt that he should be up for review at all, and
he could not answer right away. He'd had no intention of
becoming a permanent employee, so this was neither good
nor bad news to him. Instead of answering, he coughed twice.

"Are you taking medicine for that?"

"It doesn't go away, but it doesn't stop me from working
either."

"So it's not necessarily cause for concern. Even if it is contagious."

"I do feel sorry that I might be spreading it."

He didn't feel sorry at all. His boss patted him on the shoulder, looking unconvinced but also completely unconcerned, and left the changing room.

The man stamped his time card and checked the bulletin board in the office. An enormous chart that filled nearly the entire wall displayed each day's work posting. It took him a while to find his name. He was being sent to District 4.

"I guess I won't get to work with you today."

His partner, a younger employee, had appeared at his side. Each time they had been assigned to District 4, the man had swapped places with someone else.

He had not been back there since leaving. Nevertheless, whenever he got off work late at night and discarded a bag of trash in a dumpster in a dark alley, and whenever he had no trash to throw away, whenever he saw a cat slinking around the dumpster and waiting for him to leave, and whenever there was no cat, whenever he smelled something foul and did not know where it was coming from, and whenever he smelled nothing at all, whenever cumulus clouds were floating in a clear blue sky, and whenever the sky was hazy and overcast, whenever he saw a vagrant loitering near a park or subway station, and whenever he saw immaculately dressed people strolling down a sidewalk, whenever he awoke in his new apartment with its single bedroom and kitchen and bathroom, and whenever he fell asleep in that apartment, whenever he very occasionally shut off the water somewhere so he could inspect the pipes and water tank and turned it back on only to have rusty water come pouring out, and whenever clear water tainted with nothing at all came out, whenever he ate from a tray in the company cafeteria, and whenever he ate lunch in a restaurant in the neighborhood he had been sent to work in that day, whenever he saw the knife that had been set next to his plate, and whenever there was no knife, in other words, at nearly every single moment of his life, he thought about District 4.

His partner automatically started to walk away to ask their boss about switching districts, but he stopped him.

"Today's your lucky day," he said. "No one knows that district better than I do."

His partner looked puzzled at first, but when he saw the playful look on the man's face, he broke into a grin. As his partner began stuffing their tool bag with chemicals and equipment, the man let out a few hacking coughs. His partner paused and told him in a worried-sounding voice to go to the doctor. He nodded absentmindedly and lifted the bag to his right shoulder.

District 4 was festooned with banners urging flu prevention. Each time the wind blew, the stiff fabric fluttered and snapped. The man noticed a few people wearing masks, but it appeared to be due to the usual seasonal flu rather than to the virus that'd had everyone on alert. The streets were pristine, not so much as a single dropped tissue. Smoking while walking was illegal, so there weren't even the usual cigarette butts. He could not believe that those same streets had once been filled with trash and packed with single-occupant vehicles driven by people who refused to use public transportation, who ignored the traffic lights and laid on their horns nonstop and got into constant fender benders and fistfights over the pell-mell of tangled cars. Though none of it had been any fun at the time, it felt now like a joke that gets told over and over.

It had not taken long for District 4 to return to normal. It was as if the epidemic had been nothing more than a rumor. People had done their part by maintaining a semblance of daily life even amid fear and uncertainty. After the epidemic subsided, almost everyone, excepting those who had died of illness and those who had run away for fear of illness, had returned to their usual places. The misfortunes brought on by the epidemic were now little more than personal problems.

"You said you used to live around here?" his partner asked.

He'd been gazing wistfully out the car window the whole time. He nodded slowly.

"It was a small apartment building," he said. "I don't know if it's still there."

"Of course it's still there. Apartments might not survive as long as cockroaches do, but they're still good for at least thirty years. Would you like to go check it out?"

"We can't loaf or we'll be stuck working overtime."

His partner double-checked the address they'd been posted to and let out a low whistle.

"Seems it's your lucky day."

"What do you mean?"

"We're working Sixth Street. That's right nearby. We're going to pass it anyway, so I'll throw it in for you. To commemorate your visit."

The man watched quietly as his partner drove. The world outside the window looked different from what he had seen before, or what he thought he'd seen. This didn't surprise him. He felt like he had already seen everything. After a moment, they saw the street sign for where his old apartment was located. The buildings zipped past. Everything looked too alike and, making matters worse, the lack of trash in the street made it impossible for him to find the building where he had lived for only a few days. His partner slowed the car without a word and drove up and down the block several times, but he could not pick out the building. If only there had been a light fog, some trash on the sidewalk, or a bad smell coming from somewhere, he might have remembered where his old apartment was and found it right away.

"Let's just go. It's not like we're going to park and get out."

"You seem disappointed."

"I'm not disappointed. I only lived here a few days."

"But you're always talking about how good those days were."

"Well, come to think of it, now is better."

His partner looked at him and smiled, then steered the car toward their destination. According to the address, it was where the park that he had lived in was once located, but in its place now stood a megastore. The building had four levels underground, six floors aboveground, and a two-story parking garage. The first and second basement floors contained an enormous food court. The manager of the food court was the one who had called them.

"We found a rat in the food storage. The employees went nuts. Then word got out to the customers, and we've had a real problem on our hands since then."

The heavyset manager dabbed at his face with a handkerchief already damp from the sweat that would not stop dripping.

"Wasn't this area originally a park?" he asked the manager.

"That's what they say, but I don't know if it was really a park or just one big trash fire. Either way, it was covered in trash when construction began."

The manager suddenly lowered his voice and leaned in closer to the two of them.

"I don't know if you know, but wasn't all of District 4 built on an old landfill? Maybe that's why no matter how well we clean, there's a smell that never seems to go away, and we even seem to get more rats than other places. Also, it feels like the ground is sinking. It makes me nervous. The land this store was built on used to be a park, but they burned trash right next to it, and the whole place ended up filled with garbage. Lots of homeless guys, too, and rats—it was filthy! The residents couldn't take it anymore and finally asked the mayor to just get rid of the park entirely. And that trash fire . . . from what I hear, the homeless were sometimes thrown—"

The manager abruptly stopped talking and stood up straight.

"I'm sorry. Once I get to talking, it all just comes right out. Please excuse me."

The man's partner said it was okay but didn't hide the look of discomfort on his face. The man thought about the part the manager had left off. About what the vagrants did in the park and at the trash fire. In other words, what he had done.

"It still embarrasses me to think that we were all too scared to kill one little rat. Aren't you two fellows afraid?"

"If we were, how could we do this job?" the man's partner said with a laugh.

The man himself didn't say anything. He was still terrified of rats. It had scared him in the beginning to think that he was no better off than a rat, and then later, killing rats was the only way to reassure himself that he was better off, and it frightened him that he spent every free minute hunting rats in pursuit of that relief. It was terrifying to know that he'd been led down this path by a chance encounter with a single rat, and he scared himself with his retaliatory desire to annihilate the rats that refused to die no matter how strong the poison or how vicious the lash.

"Anyway, I'll leave it in your hands. If you knew exactly how much that single rat cost us in sales, you'd be shocked."

After the manager finished showing them around and returned to his office, the man left his partner to inspect the sales floor once more and headed for the enormous warehouse next to the food court. He was pretty sure that was where the trash fire had been. The warehouse was filled with the smells of different foods; some were rotting, and the rotting things left their odor on the non-rotting things. He selected a potato from a nearby crate, rubbed it against his gray jumpsuit to wipe off the dirt, and sat on the floor and slowly scraped off the peel. The cold floor made him cough and brought back his headache, but he didn't care. He bit into the flavorless potato.

"Where did you go?"

He heard his partner looking for him. He did not answer until he had swallowed every last bite of the potato. He was about to get up when he discovered a single small rat staring at him. He had no idea where it had come from. He knew that he had to defy his own fear and kill that filthy rat. If he moved as fast as he usually did, he might be able to catch it and kill it without having to use poison. But instead, he gazed in silent wonder at this rat that would find a way to survive no matter what. The rat stood still, as if debating which direction it ought to escape in. While he hesitated, the rat skillfully hid itself in the shadows near the wall, to return back along the same path it had come.

After much time had passed, following the visit to the mega-store, the man used the same method he had figured out once before to call Yujin's office. He did it on impulse. He'd been alone in the office one day when the gray telephone on the metal desk rang. It had been a long time since he'd picked up a telephone. The person on the other end asked for the contact information of one of the employees, saying they were old friends. After telling the person he could not give out that information, he felt an unbearable urge to place a call to somewhere.

Just as before, the employee in the human resources department at Yujin's workplace sounded friendly at first but soon made it clear that his inquiry was unwelcome and told the man he could not give out that number. The man told the employee that it was a long-distance international call from Country C. He added that he had lost contact with Yujin, having left their home country long ago. Just as before, the employee felt obligated to look up the phone number for him. But in the end, it could not be found. There were several employees listed by the name of Yujin, but none of them had been born in the right year or graduated from the right college. The man asked if the employee could check whether

Yujin had resigned, but the voice on the other end turned adamant again and informed him that such information could not be given out, and hung up.

Later still, he had called information, simply to hear his mother tongue again. At the operator's high-pitched insistence, he helplessly blurted out the first name that came to mind: his ex-wife's. The operator repeated her name back to him and asked which city. He hesitated for a moment and named the city district where they had lived right after they got married. After a brief pause, a recorded announcement said, "The number you are trying to reach is not in service. Please check the number and dial again." He called information again and repeated his ex-wife's name. When the operator asked which city, he named the city district where Yujin had lived. As before, he had to listen to a recording telling him that the number he was trying to reach did not exist. He tried several rounds of this, giving his wife's name and naming different places he knew. After frittering away several days at this task, he finally came across a phone number registered to her name.

For a long time, he carried the number with him on a scrap of paper everywhere he went. He knew quite well that the unfamiliar combination of numbers written on the paper could not possibly belong to his ex-wife. Nevertheless, whenever he had a free moment, he took it out and studied it, and only when the creases from where he had folded the paper were tattered and torn did he finally dial the number. It rang several times, but no one answered. When he set the phone back down in its cradle, he remembered how his ex-wife had deliberately ignored his calls for a while after their divorce, and he felt hurt all over again. The next time, he tried calling late at night. A man answered. Drawn by the familiar sound of his mother tongue, he slowly said his ex-wife's name.

"Who's calling?"

The voice on the other end sounded impatient and full of suspicion, like they might hang up immediately if the caller did not reveal himself at once. He said he was an old friend.

"She's not here right now."

He assumed from his tone that the other man was lying. The longer the other man refused to put her on the phone, the more obsessed he became with talking to her, as if the woman on the other end, this person with the same name as his ex-wife, were his ex-wife herself. He pleaded with the man, saying that he just had to speak with her. The man on the other end stayed on the phone—he must have wanted to know who this mystery caller was. But when his voice turned tearful, the man on the other end grew impatient and hung up. He dialed the number again right away, but no one answered, and when he dialed the next day, someone picked up and listened just long enough to confirm that it was his voice and then hung up. When he tried the number again a few days later, a recorded message informed him that the number he was trying to reach was no longer in service.

He dropped by his old company headquarters. Like the phone calls, he did it on a whim. He happened to be in the area on a job. The whole neighborhood had been designated as a Special Global Zone: different companies with branch offices all around the world were located there, and the business hotels nearby were booming. The pest control company he worked for serviced several hotels in the area.

Just as before, the lobby was staffed by three guards (though he could not tell if they were the same guards) all standing at ease with their hands behind their backs. He had his partner wait outside while he went in. He asked the first security guard who met his eye how he might go about meeting with one of the employees. The guard asked with a friendly smile for the name and department. He named Mol's department, but the guard tilted his head at him and pointed out the company directory posted on the wall: there was no such department. He no longer had to fill out a meeting request form, but the new system only allowed him into the building after speaking directly with an employee over the phone. He had no choice but to admit to the guard that while he did want to meet Mol, he knew nothing else about Mol other than the department he had once worked in. After going through the company directory page by page, the guard informed him that the name Mol was so common, there were seven different employees by that name. The man's pitiful expression did not waver, so the guard was kind enough to allow him to call each number in turn. He dialed all seven Mols one after the other and explained that he had been transferred there from abroad long ago. Each replied that they knew nothing about any overseas transfers. After having the exact same conversation with all seven Mols, he politely thanked the guard for his help. The guard seemed to appreciate his courteousness—he pointed to the name of the pest control company stitched on his jumpsuit and asked if he worked there. When he nodded, the guard said that the company was looking into selecting an exterminator and asked for a business card. He took a card from the front pocket of his bag and handed it to the guard, who laughed. The name on the business card read Mol. He looked at the guard and let out a hollow laugh, as if the whole thing had been a joke.

After failing at every long-distance call, he resolved not to make any more calls to anywhere or anyone. The resolution did not last long. Whenever he was on his way home late at night after work, feeling like at any moment he might come across a rat in some darkened alley, he would rush to the nearest phone booth, lit up as brightly as a lighthouse. He chose them because they were the only brightly lit things around. Inside that narrow glass box, he would pick up the receiver and speak aloud whichever names came to mind. His ex-wife's name. Yujin's name. His own name. The receiver, which made no sound, not even a dial tone, unless he inserted a coin, listened quietly to the names he spoke.

His voice echoed gently inside the glass box. Those names were his sole connection to a distant, unreachable past.

He sometimes raced off to phone booths in the middle of the day, too, whenever he was spraying the places that rats liked to travel and stumbled across one that had emerged before the rest of its colony and died. Phone booths were the only place where he could be completely alone. He called the old branch office where he used to work as well. Someone always answered before the end of the first ring. He would be too busy trying to identify their voice to say anything himself. The voice of the person on the other end was different each time, and he could never picture who it was. He did not know if this was because so much time had passed, or because he had never heard those voices before. He had watched the seasons change and return, had seen the epidemic spread like bushfire and settle into ash, had witnessed healthy new shoots sprout from that ash and grow thick and wild. And he had watched again as the threat of new epidemics were forewarned and warnings gave way to short-lived fear. But fear did not last. Those who believed that the only fallback was to remember past experience and keep a grip on reality continued to maintain their daily lives, which were so identical to their lives before the epidemic, so utterly unchanged and only slightly less comfortable now, as to negate the supposed deadliness of the virus. Meanwhile, much time had passed, which meant it only stood to reason that new employees would have been hired. While debating

who he should ask to be transferred to, he would find himself feeling bewitched by the kindness of those unfamiliar
voices, and would end up giving his own name every time.
Most asked him to repeat the name. Perhaps they thought
they had misheard him. He would carefully sound out his
name syllable by syllable only to be told, "I'm sorry, but there
is no such person."

He kept calling because he thought that if only someone
who used to know him would answer, they might say, "That
person is no longer with the company." And if that happened, he could hang up, happy in the knowledge that he
had just conversed, however briefly, with someone who knew
him. But each time he called, he was asked to repeat his
name and was told, "I'm sorry, but there is no such person."
It happened so many times that he hung up without feeling
disappointed.

If Trout had answered (once, he felt the urge to give Trout's
name instead, but in the end he gave his own name anyway),
he would have greeted him, but that never happened in all of
the calls he made. If Trout had been made branch manager
as he had hoped—as they all had hoped—then he would not
have been able to get a hold of him without going through
Trout's secretary first.

"Were you making another call?" his partner asked as he
put his dust mask back on.

"Yeah, I guess I was."

"You should just install a phone booth in your apartment."

"Can I do that?"

"Actually, your place already has one!"

His partner laughed and pointed at him. His partner had nicknamed him Booth after his habit of ducking into phone booths when they were supposed to be working or right after they were done. The man liked the nickname. The first time his partner had teased him about it, he was reminded that the word for *public phone* in his mother tongue was a homonym for *in the air*. It was true. He was a man suspended in thin air, a man airborne.

But this time he could tell from his partner's half-joking complaint that he would have to stop making calls. He fitted his industrial-strength dust mask firmly over his nose and mouth and pressed the button on the sprayer nozzle. The smell of pesticide made him cough. The coughing didn't stop, so he lifted his free hand to his masked mouth. When he did that, the sprayer hose bent toward him, and the pesticide that had been pooled inside the hose poured out onto his head and dripped down his face. His exposed skin smarted from the bitter-smelling chemicals. The smell alone was almost enough to bring tears to his eyes. But he held back the tears and set down the container of pesticide that he'd had strapped to one shoulder, removed his mask, and blew his congested nose as hard as he could. His partner gave him a sympathetic look. He smiled at his partner through tear-filled eyes and decided he would have to stop by the megastore in his old district, to pick up something for dinner.